‘So, what *is* your problem?’

‘You. *You’re* my problem. You see—’ he took a step closer ‘—while I seem to have this inability to stay away from you for long, and together we seem to have this ability to end up in an argument of some kind or another every damn time, I’m left with a real problem deciding whether to strangle you or kiss you senseless. Because you have to know as well as I do that most of this arguing comes down to one thing.’

‘And that is?’ She knew the answer before he said it.

‘It’s sexual tension. What we ended on last time is exactly what we’ve started with this time. We’re not done. We’re nowhere near done.’

Dear Reader

When meeting your first love again, Shannon Hennessey has some basic rules for you to follow:

1) Just because he's suddenly some kind of hotshot millionaire it doesn't mean he can use it as an excuse to take charge. So call him on his behaviour—every step of the way.

2) If unable to ignore that he's still sex on legs, use the fact that he still seems to be interested in you to distract him from making a mess of your life again—even if that means dirty dancing with him in front of all your friends. Work it, girl!

3) Be thankful for your secret love of sexy underwear (you just never know who might get to see it who doesn't work in the emergency room of a hospital)—because once your millionaire gets a glimpse you're guaranteed to distract him further (see point 2).

4) DO NOT go falling for him all over again—even if he does irresistible things that involve designer labels and bags of sweets—or if he spends hour after hour demonstrating the difference between sex and making love, to extremely good effect...

5) If you DO fall for him all over again, realise that to take a chance on the kind of happy ending you read about in books you may have to open a part of your soul to him. Even if it's the hardest thing you'll ever have to do…

'H's & 'K's

Trish

THE RETURN OF THE REBEL

BY

TRISH WYLIE

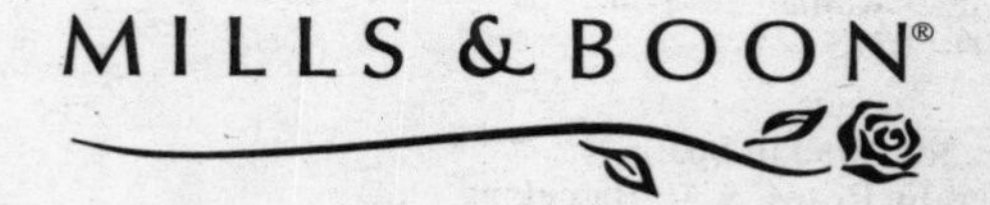

First published in Great Britain 2007
Harlequin Mills & Boon Limited,
Eton House, 18-24 Paradise Road, Richmond, Surrey TW9 1SR

ISBN-13: 978 0 263 85393 3

Set in Times Roman 10½ on 13pt
171-0707-60515

Printed and bound in Spain
by Litografia Rosés, S.A., Barcelona

Trish Wylie tried various careers before eventually fulfilling the dream of writing. Years spent working in the music industry, in promotions, and teaching little kids about ponies gave her plenty of opportunity to study life and the people around her. Which in Trish's opinion is a pretty good study course for writing! Living in Ireland, Trish balances her time between writing and horses. If you get to spend your days doing things you love then she thinks that's not doing too badly. You can contact her at www.trishwylie.com

Look out for BRIDE OF THE EMERALD ISLE
by Trish Wylie
out this month in Mills & Boon® Romance!

Recent books by the same author:

Modern Extra
BREATHLESS!
WHITE-HOT!

Mills & Boon® Romance
RESCUED: MOTHER-TO-BE
THE WEDDING SURPRISE
O'REILLY'S BRIDE
PROJECT: PARENTHOOD

For my good friend Shona—
proof-reader extraordinaire!

CHAPTER ONE

SHANNON HENNESSEY WAS just hitting that point in the morning when her coffee craving was kicking in, which meant, without her even checking her watch, that she knew it had to be almost eleven. Her craving tended to be an excellent timekeeper.

Then the front door opened with a familiar creak.

It wasn't an unusual sound, so at first she didn't even bother looking up. When she did, her usual bright smile in place for whatever familiar friendly face she might discover there, her heart stopped. *Seriously.* A miniature cardiac arrest. She even had to blink a couple of times to be sure she was seeing who she was seeing.

It just couldn't be *him!*

He stepped down into the foyer, his chin lifting, dark eyes locking with green.

And Shannon swallowed hard as inside her head she could suddenly hear—*Barry White.*

Yup, for no apparent reason—apart from the obvious one walking her way—she could hear Barry White singing in her head.

While Connor Flanaghan made a cursory examination of his surroundings with dark eyes before his gaze found hers again.

And Shannon's mouth went dry.

Oh, Lord. It was *Connor Flanaghan.*

'Hi.'

Oh, way to go with the witty opener, Shannon!

But in fairness what was she supposed to say? She wasn't prepared for this. Not now. Not here. Not when she finally had a hold of her life! After all, it was a seven-year-cycle thing, wasn't it? She'd promised herself that it was. And she was now due the good times!

Raising her hand in annoyance to tuck an errant corkscrew of long blonde hair behind an ear, she watched him walking across the room to her through narrowed eyes. How in the name of heaven did someone look that good after all this time? Couldn't he at least have aged badly? Grown a paunch? Had a receding hairline? *Anything—*

Anything at all that might have stopped the old, oh-so-familiar ache forming low in her abdomen, while a once-over-played memory appeared unbidden across the backs of her eyes. *Damn.* He'd just always been disgustingly irresistible, hadn't he?

And Barry sang in her head while a dark, impenetrable gaze remained fixed on his face as he got closer, somehow magically cementing her feet to the floor with just that silent look.

Oh, he was just too damn good-looking for his own good, wasn't he? As he got closer she recognized that look in his eyes that said he maybe knew something she didn't and was silently amused by it. Even the way he walked was full of the kind of arrogant self-confidence that came from more than just physical strength. Not that his six-foot-two, long-legged, broad-shouldered frame didn't move with more than a hint of finely tuned physical strength, but his confidence stemmed from more than that. *Yes, indeed-y.*

He probably knew that women all over the place had Barry White singing in their heads when he was around.

Less than a foot away from her, he stopped, a slow, oozing-sex-appeal smile forming on the sensual sweep of his mouth as his gaze dropped to read the message on her T-shirt.

Forcing Shannon to drop her chin for a second to check what message she was wearing that day. Of all the varying stupid things she had on T-shirts this one was at least a safer: 'Spelling Bee Runnor Up'. Lord alone knew what kind of a look she'd have earned for her favourite: '*Here I am.* Now what are your other two wishes?'

But even so, it still meant he was looking at her breasts—within two minutes of walking back into her life.

Barry was singing a little louder.

Shannon cleared her throat, waving a hand upwards to bring Connor's attention back to her eyes. 'My eyes are up here, Connor.'

He laughed, the very male sound low and deep as thick dark lashes rose, his brow furrowing with momentary curiosity. 'Sorry, do I know you?'

She sighed in resignation. The sparks in his dark eyes told her he knew rightly who she was. And he knew she knew.

They had too much history.

'Hello, Shannon.'

Man, but he still had it didn't he—that way of saying her name *just so?* And Barry could just shut up—she wasn't gonna get pulled back into the maze that was being fascinated by Connor Flanaghan. He could say her name that way as many damn times as he wanted. Shannon was *over him.*

The music stopped with a screech similar to a scratched record in her head. Ha! See—with age came control over one's raging hormones…

'What brings you to Galway?' She pinned a smile in place while her pulse continued ignoring her attempts at willing it into a slower pace.

Connor dragged his gaze from her face, looking around the room for a brief second before he locked eyes with her again, his deep baritone voice low and flat. 'I'm in Galway on business.' He paused. 'I own this place.'

Shannon laughed aloud, the sound wobbling a little nervously despite her best effort. 'No, you don't. Devenish Enterprises owns this building. I should know; it's on my lease. Nice try, though, funny guy.'

He'd always been one for a good wind-up.

Light sparkled briefly in his eyes. 'I *am* Devenish Enterprises.'

'No, you're not.'

'Yes, I am.'

'No, you're not.' Shannon shook her head in frustration as she realized how childish the level of conversation had become—she'd obviously been working with kids for too long. Any second now she'd no doubt feel the need to stick her tongue out at him. 'Frank McMahon is Devenish Enterprises. He's a big-shot millionaire property developer who owns buildings all over the country. Last I heard—you hadn't won the lottery.'

'Been checking up on me, have you?' He grinned the kind of devastating grin that had turned her knees to mush every darn time back in the day. But when she merely quirked a disbelieving brow at him, he glanced away, his voice lower as he asked, 'You still speak to Tess?'

Shannon ignored the first cheeky challenge and focused on the second question. 'Yes, we talk and e-mail from time to time—which is why I think she'd have mentioned it if your numbers came up or you suddenly made a fortune overnight. So, what are you *really* doing here? Honestly?'

It sure as hell wouldn't be because he'd been specifically looking for Shannon. Oh, no. She'd waited half her life just to have him notice her. And in the end she had taken fate into her own hands…

Yes, indeed-y, and look how karma had punished her for *that* one in the long term!

'You talk recently?' His gaze flickered briefly back to her face, searching intently, almost as if he was trying to read her mind, before he began to prowl around the large foyer, stopping to read some of the fliers on the notice-board before he looked back at her again.

Shannon had to take a moment to think about her answer. And not just because of the way he had casually leaned back against the table below the notice-board, folding his arms across his broad chest while he waited on her reply.

Silently she warned Barry to be quiet.

All right. Question. He had asked her a question. What was it again? Oh, yes. Tess. When had she last talked to her best friend of old? Erm…

She'd been so busy for months now getting settled in, putting down some roots for the first time in a long time while she got everything running smoothly and adjusted to her new surroundings, and, yes, she'd probably been so passionate about it that she'd blocked the rest of the world out. But had it really been so long since she'd spoken to her friend? With a frown, she realized—yes, it *had* been quite a while since she'd talked to her.

Something that would have to be rectified, sooner rather than later, now that Shannon had this new *visitor.*

Another thought crossed her mind. 'Has something bad happened I should know about?'

Maybe it was the genuinely concerned tone she voiced the question in, or maybe it was simply the question itself, but either way it changed something in Connor's steady gaze. So that, when he glanced away from her yet again, Shannon had to use her deep well of memories to read his familiar profile. What she saw worried her.

It was there in the tight line of his jaw, the lowered dark brows, in the way that he pursed his sensuous mouth into a thin line.

Something wasn't right here.

'Connor?' She forced herself not to allow her upper body to physically sway forwards in his general direction. Because seven years apart didn't give her any right to 'sway' anywhere near him. Not that that had stopped her before.

This 'sway' was just a reflex, nothing more. Those seven years had made plenty of changes to the person Shannon was now. Just because Connor Flanaghan had walked back into her line of vision didn't mean she would fall all over his feet again.

No matter how damn good he looked.

Had he changed his hair? She pursed her lips together while she studied it. It was shorter, hints of chestnut on the ends of the dark chocolate spikes that suggested he'd recently spent a lot of time in the sun. And he was pretty tanned too…

Shut-up-Barry!

Connor's broad shoulders lifted and fell, his chest expanding briefly as he inhaled. But instead of answering her, he unfolded his arms, pushing fluidly onto his feet before shoving his large hands deep into the pockets of his tailored trousers and glancing around the room again as he *prowled.*

And it was most definitely prowling. He had a way of moving that looked so effortless, all that restrained strength, all that silent self-control while he continued to take in his surroundings with observant eyes. He was practically predatory.

Every female hormone she possessed recognized and immediately reacted to that sheer alpha-male, leader-of-the-herd quality in him. It was positively compelling.

Shannon had to shake her head a little to clear her thoughts when he spoke again.

'So, you work here? Which one does that make you—Senior Citizens Aerobics, Potty about Pottery or Yummy Mummy Yoga?'

He'd got all that from a thirty-second glance at the noticeboard? Oh, he was *slick.*

'I lease the entire building. The bottom two floors I sublet to various groups, and I live on the third. If you're interested in any of the classes I can enrol you—' she couldn't help smiling at the glint of amusement in his eyes when he flashed a half-smile her way '—though if you're thinking of upping the rent and you're *really* the new owner of Devenish, we could just have a nice long chat about some upgrades to the plumbing and electricity instead. I have a list, as it happens…'

'As tempting as the Yummy Mummy Yoga might be, no, I don't need enrolling. I'm too busy at the minute. And we don't need to chat about the plumbing or the electricity, because the sale of this place was agreed two days ago.'

Shannon's breath caught. *'What?'*

Another shrug. And this time, despite the turn in the conversation, Shannon was suddenly struck by the way he was dressed. She had never seen Connor in a suit before, not that she could remember. Let alone in a suit that looked as if it had probably cost more than she paid in rent for the whole building per month. Suits like that one had to be made to measure, didn't they? The cut of the cloth highlighting the lean, muscled frame beneath to devastating perfection. Oh, no. That hadn't come off the peg, had it? Even if an off-the-peg one would still probably have looked just as good on him, or *off him.*

Shannon knew that, either way, he was a sensational specimen of manhood. She hadn't forgotten *anything.*

She swallowed hard.

But the suit was the first thing to persuade her that this might not be a wind-up—what he was saying might actually be true. Because the Connor she had known had been a jeans and T-shirt kind of a guy, the simplicity of the things he chose to wear only adding to his attraction back then. He hadn't had to dress to impress when he'd had an innate ability to sail through life on a combination of wit, charm and innately sexual good looks.

In a suit he was a very different male altogether. Not just appearing suave or businesslike as the suit no doubt intended, but *exuding* authority, especially on a man like Connor; he had the look of a man of power—a man in control. In fact, he really could pass as the owner of Devenish Enterprises if he wanted to, dressed like that.

If he really *was* the new owner, that would make him some kind of multimillionaire, wouldn't it?

But a man with so much money that it didn't matter to him who he trampled along the way? That wasn't the Connor Flanaghan she'd known once upon a time.

Either way, it made no difference. Whoever he was now, he wasn't the Connor she had loved, was he?

Yep, she'd sailed that ship. And it had gone down like the *Titanic*.

The thought brought a momentary sense of familiar grieflike loss into her heart. One she forced back down into its place but came out in the tight tone in her voice,

'So, you're suddenly a millionaire?'

Connor's mouth quirked. 'So it would seem.'

'Overnight?'

'It's been known to happen.'

She couldn't stop the snort of laughter that escaped., 'Yeah, sure it does. We're just tripping over millionaires in here right enough. It's a big problem for us. I can't tell you the number of Dior dresses I've been given.'

Connor sighed impatiently in response. 'It doesn't really matter how it happened, Shannon. I'm the new owner. And this place has just been sold. That's why I'm here.'

The repercussions of what he was saying began to sink into her addled mind, slowly, like water through the tiny cracks in a wall. 'Just like that? No warning? It's done and we're, what, forced to leave? *Ooh*—do we even get to pack or is this an eviction right now this minute? Do you have a nice white van outside?'

Still prowling the room, he ignored her sarcasm, answering in a businesslike tone that she had never heard from him before. 'I'm narrowing down the amount of properties on the company books, so—'

'Well, bully for you.'

He quirked a dark brow at her sharp interruption. 'Is there a problem?'

'Now, why would there be a problem?' She tilted her head to one side, the curled lock of blonde hair working loose again to bob against her cheek. 'I mean, you've just wandered in here and informed me that you're some big-shot property owner and I'm about to lose my home and my livelihood in one fell swoop. Why on earth would there be a problem with that?'

'Of course, we'll organize an alternative building for you.'

'That's big of you.'

He stopped prowling and aimed a small amused smile at her. 'Shannon. It's not that big a deal.'

Well, that was where he was wrong. It was *absolutely* a big deal. The Connor she had known might have taken the time to find that out before he wandered in with this life-changing decision already made—and it wasn't just Shannon's life either.

The building, the small community that had built up inside it, was everything to her. For the first time since her grandmother had died and left her alone in the world, she'd had a place to call home; even a hodge-podge of eclectic family to surround her.

And now Mr Millionaire was here to take it from her? There was a certain cruel irony to that…

Shannon's chin rose in defiance. 'It's a big deal to me. The Connor Flanaghan I knew would have taken the time to find that out.'

Connor studied her with his dark eyes for what felt like for ever, while Shannon did her best to swallow back the wave of anger and resentment building inside her.

This was *so* not the way she had planned on it being if she ever saw him again. But, hey, at least she couldn't hear Barry White in her head any more. Every cloud, right?

'Why?'

'Why?' Was he *kidding?*

'Yes—why? Why is it a big deal?' With his gaze still locked on hers he took one large hand out of a pocket and waved it in an arc at his side. 'It's just some crumbly, old, and, in fairness, *incredibly* ugly building. And I have no problem with helping you find an alternative. I owe you that much at least.'

She'd been about to defend the classic Victorian Gothic exterior she loved so much before he'd added the last part.

'You *owe* me?' The colour drained from her face as her hands went cold. 'What does *that* mean?'

Another shrug. 'We knew each other. Because of our history I'm prepared to make some concessions.'

Shannon stood statue still and stared at him, her heart missing several beats in her chest while she fought to find the words to express her incredulity without giving anything away.

In the ensuing silence Connor's mouth quirked, another low chuckle of laughter escaping. 'What's *that* look for?'

Shannon shook her head, turning her back on him as she opened the large daily diary on the counter behind her and silently prayed that she had misinterpreted his meaning.

'Maybe you should just go out the door and come back in again and we'll try starting this conversation over because, *really,* this is a little too surreal right now. I haven't even had my second cup of coffee yet. I can never think straight 'til I've had my second cup of coffee. So go away, come back later, and we'll start with the weather and work our way up to the difficult stuff.'

The only noise in the room for a few minutes was the tapping of one end of Shannon's pen off the wooden surface while she waited for him to say something or leave. Leave being her personal preference.

And she needed that time. That brief break from just looking at him. In order to try and calm her thoughts, to push back the momentary sense of panic that she'd felt when he said he'd 'owed' her something because of their 'history'.

Maybe if she closed her eyes and tapped her heels together three times this little nightmare would just disappear? It might be worth a try…

She almost jumped out of her skin when he touched her.

If she hadn't been wearing a T-shirt then maybe he wouldn't have touched his heated fingers against her cool, bare skin. If she hadn't still been recovering from the shock of seeing him again and everything he had told her in the space of a few minutes, then maybe the heat of that touch on her cold skin wouldn't have felt like a bolt of pure electricity.

And then maybe she wouldn't have spun round and snatched her arm from his long fingers so fast that she knocked her elbow hard off the edge of the counter.

'Damn it!'

Rocking back from him she nursed her elbow, scowling at the sharp shard of pain working its way up into her shoulder while tears immediately stung in her eyes.

It really hurt! And it was all *his* fault!

She glared venomously at him.

Connor's mouth twitched as he reached out to her again. 'Let me see.'

Shannon sidestepped him. 'No. Go away, Connor.'

'I'm not going anywhere until you let me see your elbow.' He stepped in front of her again.

So, with a smirk she lifted her hand past her shoulder to point her aching elbow at him. 'Happy now? Or do you want to kiss it better?'

His dark eyes flamed briefly and Shannon gasped.

But when he attempted to reach for her arm again and she snatched it away again, this time with an accompanying grimace, he sighed loudly.

'When did you get to be so pigheaded?'

Shannon tilted her head, mouth pouting, batting her lashes at him. 'Oh, maybe around about the same time you became a big-shot multimillionaire?'

With all attempts at helping her rebuffed he finally refolded his arms across his broad chest, tilting his head *without* pouting or batting his lashes. He didn't need to do anything more than stare at her to get his point across. He was losing patience. Fast.

And his words confirmed it. 'Are you done with your little tantrum now?'

Shannon glared harder.

While he lifted his arm slightly, shrugging back the end of his sleeve to check his watch. ''Cos I have another meeting in a half hour, but I can wait a few more minutes for you to calm down if that'll help any.'

She opened her mouth to say how very sweet that was of him, only to have him step closer so that she was trapped between the counter and his large body.

Uh-oh.

When he spoke again, his voice was lower, deeper; it held a more determined edge. So that she was completely distracted from sarcasm and instead mesmerized by his sheer maleness. Had he been this overwhelming up close before? She didn't remember that part.

Barry White started singing in her head again.

'I could have just sent you a letter, Shannon. But when I

saw whose name was on the lease I decided to come and talk to you face to face, out of respect. This isn't personal, selling the building, it's just business. And I'll make sure there's a place for you to move to. I already told you that. There are plenty of other buildings in better places where you could run all these little things you do to amuse yourself.'

Shannon scowled, opening her mouth again, this time to discuss the meaning of the word 'patronizing' with him.

But Connor was on a roll. 'Believe it or not, I didn't come here to have a fight with you. I actually *wanted* to see you.'

Her eyes widened. 'Why?'

This smile was slow, smouldering, sensuous. And whatever else might have changed about him, Shannon recognized *that* smile. He was turning on the charm. *For her.* Seven years too late.

'I've always been curious why you left without saying goodbye. Don't you think that was a little rude of you?'

'You're here to tell me off for my manners after *seven years?* You've got to be *kidding* me!'

She watched as his eyes made an intensive study of her, from the top of her head, to each of her eyes, along her nose, finally resting on her lips. The lips she involuntarily swiped with the tip of her tongue before parting them to draw in several short gasps of air.

'I just thought that, considering what happened between us, you might have taken five minutes to say cheerio before you flew out of the country. It's what *I'd* have done.'

Shannon swallowed hard. 'After—*what*—happened?'

His gaze lifted, ever so slowly, locking with her wide-eyed stare as he leaned his head a little closer, his voice dropping to pillow-talk level. 'Was it that easy to forget? I always thought the first time was supposed to be an unforgettable experience?'

Her breath caught. *O-h-n-o!*

'You knew it was me?'

He chuckled, the dimples in his cheeks creasing. 'Of course I knew. You knew I knew. It was all part of the game that night. There's no way you could have thought that disguise *worked?*'

Well, actually…

Despite the ache in her elbow, Shannon lifted both arms, reaching her hands out to his chest to push hard, a wave of almost adolescent humiliation driving her to get as far away from him as possible.

'Get away from me.'

She was halfway across the room before he spoke again, a hint of humour still in his voice. 'We're not done discussing the building and where you're moving to.'

Shannon laughed sarcastically. 'Oh, we're done, believe me. And there's no discussion to be had about this building, because I have a long lease and I won't be moving anywhere.'

'The sale is already agreed. It'll take approximately six weeks to go through the solicitors. So you don't really have a choice. And the next owners might not be so considerate about where you end up—unless you have some history with one of them too.'

Son-of-a—

She swung round and advanced back to him with gritty determination. She wasn't some naïve teenage girl any more. And the sooner he realized that, the better.

'I have a choice all right. I'll fight you for this place if I have to, because it's not just a crumbly old ruin to me. But I don't expect you'd understand that any more than you understand how lower than low it was of you just now to bring up what happened way back then. *Believe me,* if I had to go back I'd do things a lot differently.'

His humour disappeared instantaneously. 'Including what happened with me?'

The answer to that was swift, borne from the gaping wound she still carried buried way, way deep inside.

'*Especially* what happened with you. That was the biggest mistake of my life. And if I could go back in time it would never happen!' She looked him down and back up, her next words enunciated with distinct iciness. 'Never in a million years.'

The air in the foyer went chilly. Arctic, in fact.

'Well, then, I've just had any questions I had about the way you left answered, haven't I?' This time when he smiled there was no hint of his earlier humour, his voice deadly calm. 'You'll get written confirmation of the sale in the next few days along with a list of alternative buildings. Choose one.'

'Don't bother sending anything. *I'm* not moving.'

Nodding, he glanced down at his watch again. 'Fine, then. Have it your way.'

Even after the doors had creaked shut behind him, Shannon still stood in the one spot, hands on her hips, head tilted back, as she took long deep breaths to try and calm herself.

Connor Flanaghan.

But as the deep breathing gradually brought her rapidly beating heart under control, the bare facts of their confrontation rose to the fore.

She had to stop him.

But could she, Shannon Hennessey—who had never once fought to stay somewhere before—stand up and fight for the place she now called home?

Yes, she could and she would. With whatever weapons she had in her mature arsenal.

Connor Flanaghan had a heap of trouble headed his way!

CHAPTER TWO

WHY WAS IT that, on top of everything else, he had thought it would be a good idea to go see Shannon Hennessey again?

Connor was still asking himself that question long after he'd left her. After he had been to three different meetings and looked over five buildings and was finally hauling off his tie in his suite in Galway's top hotel.

Pacing around the large, perfectly ordered room, he went over it in his mind.

Her name on the lease had been the last thing he'd expected to see. And, yes, curiosity had probably had a hand in him visiting her personally rather than sending an agent as he normally did.

But there'd been a time in his life when Shannon had almost been a part of the furniture. Always there, always in the background, so shy at the beginning, but then funny and cute and bright—the stereotypical girl next door. Swiftly followed by the time when he had noticed she was growing up, 'debating' everything with him, challenging him, flirting with him—treading closer and closer to that fine line between friendship and something more.

Until the one night he had let her play her somewhat dangerous game through to its logical conclusion.

But she was something altogether different now, wasn't she? Oh, yeah, now she was all grown-up. It had been no teenager or naïve virgin that had looked at him the way she had that afternoon. It took a fully grown woman to look at a man that way, with heavy-lidded eyes that had darkened in colour to a deep emerald-green, heating his blood faster than standing in front of an open flame ever would have. With just that look, a swipe of her full mouth with the pink end of her tongue, and he'd had a dozen memories from that one night with her bounce straight into the front of his mind.

Through every one of his afternoon appointments he'd still been able to see her face, hear her voice, mentally visualize that damn lock of hair of hers that constantly worked loose.

Yep, she'd left him angry and sullen for the rest of the day, because, if nothing else, his ego didn't appreciate her bitterness about that one night.

He paced up and down in the room, restless in the same soul-deep way he had been for weeks now. The root cause of it was easy to pin down, but the added complication of seeing Shannon again and the associated long ago memories that came with that…

Well, that had been an added complication he could have done without.

And yet practically the first thing he had done was go see her and bring up the subject of that one night. Maybe it had been crass of him, poorly handled. Okay, he would possibly have to admit to that. Shannon then throwing at him the fact that she wished it had never happened had maybe only been what he deserved as a result.

But it didn't make him any the less resentful of her reaction. And, little did she know it, she'd picked the wrong time to make him resentful.

The shrill sound of a mobile phone drew him out of his dark brooding, forcing him to take a moment to search the pocket of the jacket he had thrown to one side. But a quick glance at the screen simply made him scowl all the harder while he sighed and let it ring out.

He didn't want to talk to Rory. Not yet.

What he *wanted* was a drink someplace noisy with a crowd of people who wouldn't know him and enough pretty women to take his mind off the one woman.

What he *didn't want* in the first place he found was to see Shannon again. Was someone, somewhere, just hell-bent on keeping him in a foul mood? If they were then they were doing a very good job.

She was dancing on a small wooden dance floor to one side of the room, with a man way too 'pretty' in Connor's mind. That was her type now, was it? Somehow she'd never seemed the kind of girl to be easily swayed by someone so fashion-conscious.

But if Connor had been remembering only a half hour ago the girl next door she used to be, then the sight of her matching her lusciously curved body's moves with the tall man's only confirmed his thoughts of her being all grown-up now. And then some.

Leaning an elbow on the long polished bar, he nodded to the barman and placed his order, flashing a smile at the woman who was turning with her own drinks in hand, before he leaned back, one foot resting on the brass rail raised slightly off the floor, and continued watching Shannon through hooded eyes.

If she kept dancing like that then every red-blooded man in the room would soon be doing the same thing, wouldn't they?

And she'd have no one to blame but herself for the swarm of attention that might bring her as the night went on and alcohol clouded the judgement of those males' good manners. Would 'pretty boy' step up and fend them off—defending his territory, seeing off the competition?

Somehow Connor didn't think he looked the type.

All right, so there had been a time in Connor's life when he'd have had an avid appreciation for the kind of blatant sexual confidence in a woman that would bring that kind of trouble to his door. But this was *Shannon*.

And he found he didn't appreciate the exhibitionist in her quite the same way as he had with other women. If anything, it was like a red rag to a bull. He might just have to see for himself if 'pretty boy' was up to the task of some healthy competition…

As if in challenge, the man wrapped an arm around her waist, his fingers splaying against the skin revealed between her short black top and the waistband of her tight jeans, while he tilted his chin to watch as she brought her pelvis in against his hip, moving in a way that only had one point of reference off a dance floor that Connor could think of.

But he couldn't stop watching. He was a red-blooded male after all. The only thing that set him apart from all the other red-blooded males was that he had experience of what it felt like to have her body wrapped around his, to be buried deep inside her while her body clamped around his hard length as she fell over the edge.

On that one night she was so damn keen to forget.

With a quick flick of her head, her long blonde hair cascaded over one bare shoulder, the errant corkscrew curl immediately coming back to rest against her cheek. Then, with a smile on her lips, she glanced up. And her sparkling green eyes found his across the room.

Connor nodded his head once in acknowledgement. He didn't look away, didn't smile. He just continued to watch as she moved her hips again, her arms hanging back a little behind her body as her shoulders moved from side to side—the movement pushing her breasts up and forwards.

Two minutes.

Yep. That was all he was giving her. And then he was gonna walk right on over there and tap her partner on the shoulder. To see, just out of curiosity, how she might react to that. If she would fight him off before he could remind her of why singling him out as her first lover shouldn't be something she regretted doing. Or to see if she would remember how well their bodies had fitted, a little reminder of how they had moved and *could* move together.

After all, it wasn't as if she had complained at the time, not that Connor recalled…

Oh, yeah, he'd dance with her all right, he'd let her move her hips in against his side while he waited to see if her emerald eyes would darken the way they had when she'd looked at him that afternoon.

Only this time round they'd play the game *his* way.

But before he counted down the minutes she leaned up to speak into her partner's ear as the music changed, kissing him briefly on the cheek before she extricated herself from his hold and walked towards Connor with a tantalizingly confident sway of her hips.

She flashed him a brief look from the corner of her eye before standing on tiptoes beside him, her hand rising to run through the long curls of hair so they were off her forehead, leaning across the bar with a killer smile to order a drink, the barman smiling in blatant appreciation at her.

Connor tossed money onto the polished surface in front of her—taking care of her drink—then leaned back again to survey the crowd. Silently waiting to see what she would do next. Telling himself he'd take an apology for the way she'd been earlier, any time she felt ready to hand it out. He could still be a good guy when he put his mind to it…

He smiled at another passing female who smiled appreciatively at him on her way past with a friend, lifting his beer to take a long drink, while, glass in hand, Shannon turned round and mimicked his stance, surveying the crowd with her back against the bar.

Eventually he couldn't resist asking, 'Come here often?'

'It's one of our favourite places, actually, within staggering distance of home. Why, are you planning on selling *here* too?'

'I don't own it.' Ignoring her sugary-sweet tone, Connor lifted his bottle to his mouth again. 'You and your boyfriend can dance here to your heart's content.'

'Not that it's any of your business, but he's not my boyfriend. I'm not his type.'

He glanced at her from the corner of his eye, a small smile on his mouth. 'Prefers brunettes, does he? Man after my own heart, then.'

'Nope.' She quirked an arched brow in challenge as she turned her body towards him, her head tilting forwards a little so he could hear her lowered voice above the music. 'I'm not quite *man* enough for him, if you get my drift. He'd like *you* though, if you want an introduction?'

Connor couldn't help it; he laughed. Shaking his head as

he turned towards her, his elbow on the bar, he said, 'Oh, I think we both know that won't be necessary.'

Shannon shrugged off the innuendo, literally, eyeing him again from beneath long lashes. 'Well, I wouldn't know what else might have changed about you lately, would I?'

'Many, *many* things may have changed but that isn't one of them.' He leaned his face a little closer, watching triumphantly as her lashes flickered, her gaze on his mouth as he spoke. 'Trust me.'

There was a long silence while her eyes slowly rose until her gaze locked with his. The emerald-green taking on the darker shade he had planned on seeing when he danced with her.

She wasn't as immune to him as she'd like to think she was, was she? And that, coupled with the recent evidence of her dance moves, was more than enough encouragement. So he grinned widely, and winked at her.

Shannon laughed. 'No, some things obviously haven't changed.'

He continued grinning, even after she turned to face the bar again. And it felt good. Better than good. In fact he couldn't remember the last time when the mess of his life had been put to the back of his mind long enough for him to play a little with a woman. Even briefly. And with someone who less than a few hours ago had been so obviously determined they didn't want to play. Not with him, anyway.

Which made her *a challenge.*

Maybe persuading her to change her mind about regretting him might be exactly the kind of welcome distraction he needed after all, for a while anyway.

His phone vibrated in the pocket of his jeans and he reached in to retrieve it, the screen lighting up as he checked the number, briefly illuminating his face while Shannon turned to watch him.

He wasn't grinning by the time he turned it off.

Shannon was still watching as he pushed it back into a pocket. 'Avoiding some poor lovelorn woman?'

'Not this time. It's just Rory.'

The tension in his voice was obvious, causing Shannon to frown in confusion as she asked, 'As in Rory your big brother Rory?'

'That would be the one.'

'How is he?'

The beer bottle froze an inch from his mouth. 'I wouldn't know.'

Which only seemed to confuse Shannon all the more. 'Well, I could be wrong. But answering the phone might help with that, don't you think?'

When he looked at her face his eyes were dark, his expression grim and Shannon immediately knew it was meant as a 'butt out'.

Even before he added the firmly voiced, 'Leave it be, Shannon.'

She lifted her chin in response.

'So, no Senior Citizens Aerobics tonight?'

'I don't take the aerobics sessions.' With a shake of her head, tossing her hair over one shoulder, she took the lifeline afforded with his swift change of subject. It wasn't as if it were really any of her business anyway, so why should she care?

'I run a Tumblin' Tinies franchise for kids from eighteen months to ten years old, if you must know. And I do the reading group we have so the mothers can do their yoga classes in the mornings.'

'The *Yummy* Mummies? I have to say there's a certain element of fascination in the idea of good-looking women who can…*flex*…'

Shannon ignored the return of that silently teasing light in his dark eyes. 'I'll just bet there is in a mind like yours. But, yes, that's the ones. If they know the kids are happy they're more likely to enjoy some time of their own. So I do story time with the kids.'

'I don't remember that from the notice-board.'

'Well, that's a shame, 'cos we run a quiz on what's on the notice-board once a week. Winner gets a free yoga session.'

'You just made that up, didn't you?'

Shannon nodded. 'Yes, I did.'

Silence descended between them again until Connor took a breath and dived in on a bigger issue.

'You know, there was a time when we used to be able to get along without this much effort, if I recall. And I know we may possibly have gotten off to a bad start today—'

She shrugged. 'I liked you better when I knew you before—that's all. But then, in fairness, you'd never tried to make me homeless back then. And, anyway, this isn't us not getting along, not yet. You'll know when it is.'

Connor's eyes were still studying her as she looked around the rapidly filling bar. She didn't have to look up at his face to confirm it. She could feel it, as surely as she could probably have calculated to the very millimetre the distance between their two bodies. It was a senses thing, she supposed. But it was also a very basic-awareness-on-a-very-sensual-level thing, which both excited and frustrated her, in equal measure. He was temptation on legs, not a doubt about it.

Even so, she really *didn't* want to like him again if she could at all avoid it. She'd have to keep her wits about her if she was going to take him on to save her precious building…

And liking him might lead to her getting sidetracked.

But she hadn't come out tonight to play games with him, or have another argument with him. She hadn't come out with the intention of seeing him at all. She'd come out to enjoy herself with her friends, to *forget* about meeting the all new, not-necessarily-improved Connor.

The best laid plans…

'So, how was America?' he asked nonchalantly.

Her stomach flipped over and felt distinctly as if it hit the floor. *Hard.*

All right, so it was a logical question. The last time Connor had known her that was where she'd been headed. There was no way on God's green earth he could know what had happened when she was there.

So she took a breath, forcing a calm tone into her voice. 'It was great. I learnt a lot on the courses I did.'

'How long have you been home?'

'A year—after eighteen months in London—but I like Galway; we're a good fit for each other.'

When he went quiet she risked another sidewards glance to confirm that he wasn't questioning her because he knew something. Even when she knew he couldn't. Not without being psychic.

And there he was, large as life and twice as damn sexy without even trying, lounging laconically against the bar in the more familiar jeans-and-dark-shirt ensemble that had always had her drooling from a distance when she was old enough to know what it was she appreciated about him. Still studying her with his dark eyes, which unnerved her even more than his knowing anything could have.

'What?'

Connor shook his head. 'Nothing. I was just thinking.'

'Well don't make any effort on my behalf.'

With a smirk he reached over to leave his empty bottle on the bar, his arm accidentally brushing briefly against the side of her breast. And it took every ounce of self-control in her possession for Shannon not to flinch as her eyes locked with his.

He knew he had done it.

It was as clear as day to her that he knew what he had done, from the flash of awareness that crossed his dark eyes and the lazy smile that followed. He was silently challenging her to call him on it too! Thing was, what he maybe didn't realize was that that accidental touch had awakened a hundred memories in her mind and in her body, and allowed her to recognize that flash of awareness in his eyes for what it was: *sexual awareness.*

Maybe she wasn't the only one hearing Barry White. And *that* had to be something she could work with…

Shannon had seen that look in his eyes before. She'd even played up to it. In the past the way he had touched her hadn't been at all unintentional or accidental, it had been slow and deliberate, an awakening for Shannon—a long lesson in physical pleasure that she had never forgotten.

She would never have wanted there to be someone else her first time. Not then. She just hadn't known there would be consequences—if she *had*…

Connor smiled for another moment, but when she refused to rise to the bait he took a different approach. 'Tess was worried about you, you know. That time when you were ill in the States.'

Shannon's stomach somersaulted again. 'Ill?'

'Yes, she said you collapsed and had to go into hospital for a while.'

'Oh, that.' She damped her tongue along her dry lips and smiled through the lie. 'I had heatstroke. You know us blonde Irish girls and the sun.'

'Still, it was a long way from home to be sick and on your own.'

'I didn't have a home any more, Connor. Not after my nan died. And, anyway, everyone has something they have to get through on their own at some time or other. That's life.'

'Yes, it is.' He turned and looked out over the crowd.

A thought occurred to her. 'Is that why you're avoiding Rory? Because you have something you have to deal with alone? Or did you get in another one of those dumb ass fights with him?'

The Fighting Flanaghans they'd all been known as growing up. Four brothers completely devoted to each other who'd nevertheless spent half their adolescence arguing with each other over the most ridiculous things. And even now the memory made her smile a small smile.

But Connor merely shot her another warning glance in response.

So Shannon sighed. 'Right, I get it, you don't want to talk about it. Well, maybe I should just go get my good friend Mario to keep you company, then. He'd love that.'

'Uh-uh. I'm just fine with you to keep me company.'

Flattering and all as that was, Shannon was rapidly running out of safe topics to talk to him about. So, she ran a quick summary through her mind: he obviously didn't want to discuss whatever his problem was with his brother, she didn't want to start a row with him in public about the building issue until she had all her facts, and her being ill in America was a definite no-go zone.

Which left Shannon surrounded by choices between: a) a web of half-truths, b) dangerous topics of conversation or c) just standing still allowing the air to crackle between them while she played with the idea of using some of that sexual awareness in the here and now to her advantage.

Decisions, decisions.

'It's been unusually warm this summer, hasn't it?'

Connor smiled down at her with the kind of smile that reminded her of a time when they'd been friends without so much effort. 'And there we are—reduced to talking about the weather.'

'Well, you don't want to talk about Rory and I'm in no mood to talk about the building we're going to go to war over, so that doesn't leave us with much, does it?'

'So, dance with me.'

'What if I don't want to dance with you?'

'Tough.'

It was too late, already he was taking control, removing the glass from her hand, setting it on the bar behind her before he tangled his long fingers with hers and tugged, hard, forcing her forwards. He then looked over his shoulder as their feet hit the wooden floor, to inform her with gleaming eyes, 'Now that I've seen you have some moves it seems only fair you try them out on someone who *does* like women.'

O-h-h no. The only reason she let loose with Mario was because she knew he wouldn't read anything into it. He was 'safe'. She didn't go around dancing that freely with *every* man she met—not unless she actually planned on…

Well—with Mario she could lose her inhibitions, could

close her eyes and succumb to the sheer sexuality of a throbbing beat and a sensual rhythm. It was liberating, exhilarating, a small chance to be completely free for a few minutes.

With Connor it would be foreplay.

In fact the very thought of moving her pelvis in against him the way she had with Mario had her body heating up in ways and places it hadn't done in what felt like a long, *long* time!

This was a bad idea.

She needed a game plan before she stepped in the ring with Connor Flanaghan. A damned detailed one too!

She tried to shake her hand free. But Connor had always been stronger than her physically, and with another tug he had her hauled forwards against his body, his free hand snaking around her waist, fingers splaying against her skin to add just enough pressure so that she was held tight all along the hard length of him from thigh to chest as he began to move them in time to the music.

Shannon almost moaned aloud. Oh, Barry White had been right all along. This was *good.*

Her traitorous curves automatically fitted in against lean male muscle. And the joint movement of their bodies created friction on the most basic sexual level, pebbling her nipples harder against the lace of her bra, building a slowly widening knot of tension in her abdomen, sending a wash of moisture to her core.

Her breathing increased.

And then her eyes rose, slowly, moving from button to button on his shirt, lingering briefly on the column of his neck before she studied his mouth. His sculpted mouth with its wider lower lip—the mouth that had once kissed her lips, her neck, her breasts, the soft skin of her inner thigh…

She had to swallow down another low moan before she protested again. 'Connor—'

He held her firm when she struggled against him. 'Shush. You don't want to cause a big scene in this crowd, now, do you?'

When she looked into his eyes he had that same dark gaze that sparkled with knowing—he *knew* what he was doing to her. He knew and he was positively triumphant about it, *goddamn it!*

Tearing her gaze away, she pursed her lips together as she tried to think of another way of getting out of her predicament. She was actually fairly sure, if she did cause a big scene, she could get him kicked out. After all, she'd been coming to this place for a long time. It was her local haunt.

And one glance over his shoulder told her what she already knew—that her friends were more than aware that she was dancing with someone they had never seen before, which meant they would automatically keep an eye on her. And not *just* out of curiosity. It was something they all did for each other.

Though, in fairness, the sight of three thumbs being pointed upwards didn't give her much confidence in them as potential rescuers.

She chanced another look into his eyes. And her brain suddenly started to function.

Wait a minute. Why was she looking for a way out? Surely this was her chance to up the ante? If she was gonna go to battle with him then she couldn't go into it with him, knowing he already had an advantage over her physically. She couldn't let him think he could bend her to his will because she apparently still *wanted him.* What she needed to do was show him she was no naïve teenager any more. Hell, no. She was all grown-up now. Maybe it was about time he understood that.

So she tossed her hair back over her shoulder again, leaning back a little against his arms as she damped her lips, caught her lower lip between her teeth, smiled seductively as he watched the movement.

And for good measure she moved her pelvis across his, sliding back and forth until she heard his sharp intake of breath and felt his body go rigid.

Touché, Connor Flanaghan. Your move.

Her eyebrows quirked in challenge.

Connor's head descended slowly, until his clean shaven cheek was close to hers, musky male scent filling her nostrils as he grumbled into her ear, 'You know, they say when a couple can dance together like this it means they're compatible in other areas.'

Shannon leaned back, her voice low. 'Are you serious? That line gets you laid? *Really?*'

He angled his face above hers, his warm breath washing over her cheeks as he looked at her with hooded eyes, 'You'd be surprised.'

'Well—' she angled her face the opposite way, so that when she rocked forward a little and stood on her toes her mouth was inches from his, her eyes focused on the small distance between control and giving in to temptation '—on behalf of womankind everywhere, I am officially embarrassed that line worked for you.'

Connor smiled a lazy smile. 'Ah, but it's not really a line; it makes perfect sense. Both have to do with natural rhythm, working with the way your partner moves, adjusting the give—and the take—to make things better for each other. If you can synchronize on a dance floor then it makes sense that things are much better when—'

Whoa—and he could stop right there! She'd got it! And she needed to stay in equal control here, didn't she? So, with a cooling deep breath she leaned her head back again. 'I get the picture.'

Vividly and in Technicolor as it just so happened. Even accompanied with some bright sparks of multicoloured light when she closed her eyes as her lower abdomen came into contact with the beginnings of a rather impressive erection, and her body immediately flooded in readiness.

O-h-h—if she was going to play this game she really needed to get her responses under control, didn't she?

Instead of picturing hot, sweaty sex while her eyes were still closed.

'But then we already know we're compatible in that area, don't we, *Sunshine?*'

Her eyes flew open. He had used her nickname from the 'good old days' when she had been head over heels about him—when the very sound of that word had been interpreted as an endearment rolling off his silver tongue. And it immediately reminded her of a time when she'd had no control at all around him.

He played dirty!

His smile grew when her eyes narrowed in warning. 'I know you remember as much as I do, even if you want to try so desperately to forget it—which I really don't think you do, deep down. Not really. Maybe what we should do is try it again, just to see if it's as good a second time. You've obviously picked up some moves.' He leaned a little closer. 'I even have some new ones myself. And when you're crying out my name this time, you might find you don't regret crying it out the first time round either.'

Shannon gasped. 'Oh, well, you can just be a complete bastard when you put your mind to it, can't you?'

The arm around her waist became a steel band, his expression went dark, even his mouth twisted as he answered in a dangerously low tone, 'You have no idea how right you are.'

Shannon struggled to get free, then froze and decided instead to go on the offensive. 'You know what really got to me the most all afternoon, thinking about you knowing it was me that time? It's that you played along. The whole way through you never once felt the need to say you knew. Now just why might that be, do you think?'

He laughed. He damn well laughed out loud!

'Aw, c'mon, Shannon! You knew I knew. Pretending I didn't was all part of the game.'

He might as well have slapped her; the sense of humiliation was just *that* strong. Because he really *had* known it was her all along, hadn't he? Not only that—but he had thought it was all some big sexual game to her! He had played along for the sake of an opportunity for some hot sex! Despite her complete belief that she had seduced him into a fantasy night of memorable romance.

Which it had been. *For her.*

She'd been *so* naïve back then! So wrapped up in a romance and a happily ever after that hadn't existed. It had taken real life to teach her that one, hadn't it?

And now, thanks to Connor, she got to feel a little of that pain all over again. Slicing through her now as agonizingly as it had when she'd been alone and dealing with the aftermath of her *naïveté.*

What a bastard!

Connor leaned back in, his cheek against her cheek as his deep voice tickled against her ear. 'It was the most amazing night—don't you remember? I used to have seriously hot dreams about it after you left. I never knew that being seduced by a woman in a fantasy outfit could be so…*erotic*.'

Then his head turned a fraction, his lips brushing oh-so briefly against the sensitive skin below her ear as he spoke in a stage whisper. 'You were beautiful. A little nervous at first maybe, but then you just let yourself get lost in the moment, didn't you? And you were sexy as hell. I've never forgotten. The way you moved, the sounds you made, how you cried out when you came. *Any* of it.'

Shannon closed her eyes. It was just the absolute worst form of torture she'd ever been subjected to—laced with a bitter sweetness that tore her in two.

'It wasn't a game! You were never supposed to know it was me.'

He chuckled again. 'A mask and a cheap wig weren't gonna stop me from knowing it was you. I knew your scent. It was unmistakably you. Still is, as it happens; it's on you now. A combination of flowers and a hint of something fresh that always said Shannon Hennessey was nearby. You *chose* to make it a fantasy night—I just followed your lead.'

Perfume had given her away?

'Let go of me.'

Standing statue still in his hold, she refused to allow him to continue swaying their bodies, her eyes open and fixed on the open door across the busy bar. 'Let me go, right this minute. Or—I swear—I'll yell so loud my good friends the bouncers will knock you into next week. And I'll grin as it happens.'

Connor's large body went rigid for a moment before he took a step back, releasing her at a torturously slow pace along the way.

While Shannon stared up at his hooded eyes, her cheeks burning as her pulse continued beating erratically with a combination of arousal and anger. 'You don't know who I am now, any more than I know who you are. And quite frankly, I'm not sure I *want* to know the new you or experience any of your *new moves.* I may have been crazy enough about you seven years ago to want you to be my first time, but right this minute I dislike who you are just enough to never want to set eyes on you ever again.'

Connor's dark eyes flared as he stepped forwards, his wide chest an inch away from the rapid rise and fall of her breasts. 'Let's just take a second here and look back at who it was set up that little seduction scene all those years ago, shall we?'

'And then let's look at who played along with it right up to the end and never once let on he knew! But then maybe no-strings-attached sex was your thing? It suited you just fine to pretend you didn't know who it was underneath you!'

His mouth pursed briefly into a sharp line. 'It was what *you* wanted or it would never have happened! *Trust me.*'

The hissed words washed over her flushed cheeks as she fought to hold back angry tears. 'No. All I wanted at the time was *you!* I was just too young and too damn stupid to know any better, *obviously.* There were probably a half-dozen others who would have been a better choice!'

After a cursory flicker of his eyes over her face, he took a breath and leaned his face closer still, his mouth a mere whisper above hers while he locked eyes with her.

'If it was me you wanted, then you got your wish, didn't

you? No matter what kind of a person I was underneath. Well, you know what they say about being careful about what you wish for.'

While she stood gaping, he angled his head and added, 'What you should maybe remember for future reference is that no one is what they might like to think they are. Under that girl-next-door image of yours was an incredibly sexual woman, waiting to test out what she was capable of. It was just fortunate for you that you picked me. It could have been *much* worse.'

'Not from where I'm standing right this minute it couldn't.'

His thick dark lashes lowered as he looked down to where his mouth almost touched hers, then rose as he searched her eyes. 'Go ahead and forget it ever happened, if you can. I don't intend ever forgetting. You'll just have to learn to deal with knowing that every time you look at me, won't you? Because every time I look at you it'll be what I'm thinking of.'

'Well, it won't be what I'm thinking of when I look at you—' she almost spat the lie up at him '—so you'll just have to learn to deal with that. Because I'm no naïve little virgin any more, Connor. I'm a fully grown woman. If you thought last time was amazing—well, you just go ahead and have a little think about how much more amazing it could be with someone who actually knows what she's doing. *Then* remind yourself that the only reason you'll never get a chance to find out what it would be like is because you've turned into a complete and utter ass!'

And with that she turned, her head held high, and her hips swaying purposefully as she walked away from him.

CHAPTER THREE

THE LITTLE COMMUNITY that had built up within the walls of the building Shannon leased from Devenish wasn't long in gathering a head of steam and forming a committee.

It was what peaceful people did in times of trouble. They got together in a room to argue about what they should do next…

'I say we should get a petition together.'

'A petition isn't going to make a blind bit of difference to a company like Devenish. I say we do a sit-in protest.'

'A naked sit-in, like in the sixties? *I'm in.*' Mario winked across at Shannon.

A tiny grey-haired woman tapped her walking stick on the old wooden floor. 'We should chain ourselves to the railings outside!'

'Brieda, there aren't any railings outside.'

'Well, we have to do *something.*'

Silently, all eyes in the room swung in Shannon's direction. And she sighed in resignation. She really didn't want to do this right now. Not since she had read her e-mails that morning and found a reply from Tess, Connor's sister.

But since she had put a note on the notice-board about the sale of the building there had been a constant stream of people wanting to know what they could do to help and she knew she had no choice but to deal with it.

Even though she now had other things running rings round her mind.

'Well, in the meantime we have the lease agreement. That should buy us some time. But we'll need a solicitor to fight our case and that won't be cheap.'

'We could run some fund-raisers—get everyone who uses the building involved?'

'A sponsored walk maybe?'

'We could run a fête, bake cakes and have a tombola.'

Shannon raised her fingers to rub against her throbbing temples. They all meant well, she knew that, and she loved every one of them for loving the place as much as she did, really she did. That was the real problem for her, you see; she had fallen in love with the building the day she had set eyes on it—it had called to her. Within its walls she had made a place to call home for the first time in years. But, more importantly, in return it had supplied her with the makeshift family that now surrounded her; a family that would rely on her to find a way out of this current dilemma—regardless of just who that put her up against.

Shannon had a responsibility to do right by them. To make an effort to keep the place they all loved. And somehow, having others to fight for instead of just herself almost made it easier for her to stand her ground against Connor.

If it just didn't feel like such a very personal battle. If it just wasn't against someone she had once loved. But the very fact she knew him meant she should be able to do more, didn't it? And they needed her to think of *something.*

'I'm not sure that that'll be enough. Solicitors cost a lot of money these days,' Shannon said.

Her unguarded remark led to several crestfallen faces, and guilt immediately racked her in waves. 'But it would certainly be a start,' she added.

When she smiled encouragingly the room became a hum of voices again, until she had to clear her throat to be heard. 'What we need to do is find something about the history of this place that might get it listed as being of historical interest. Then at least it can't be torn down.'

It was a shot in the dark, she knew that. But immediately there was another flurry of loud conversation, and while her eyes fixed on Mario's proud expression as he walked towards her she didn't notice the door to the room opening.

Until Mario hissed down at her, 'Isn't that the hottie from the bar?'

Her gaze flew to the door where Connor was studying the crowd with a somewhat bemused expression. And her breath caught in her chest at the sight of him.

Because he had been right. Every damn time she looked at him she would *know.* And she hated him for it.

Large frame dominating the low doorway, he searched the room with a flickering gaze and Shannon, mimicking his search, was stunned to realize that no one seemed to have noticed his arrival. How could they miss him?

Because much as she hated him—he looked *sensational.* Dressed in another expensive, gorgeously cut dark suit with a crisp white shirt unbuttoned at the neck, his hair spiking in all directions and a hint of dark shadowed stubble on his chin—he had that 'I'd be great in bed' look that had caught her imagination so long ago.

And even more recently than that.

Only now she resented him for looking that way. Because

she didn't want to still be so aware of how he looked or to remember just how great he was in bed. And since they had danced and he had lightly suggested they try repeating the experience for some kind of comparison, despite her best efforts she'd been able to think of little else. Regardless of what she had said to him in the heat of the moment.

And it was a lie that had led to a distinct lack of sleep after she left him—which had led to even more thinking.

One of those thoughts being that their confrontation had killed every romantic notion she'd ever possessed about him. He had taken that one fantasy night and scrumpled it up like waste paper.

During the endlessly silent hours when she hadn't been able to sleep, she had steadily built a burning hatred for him for the constant, never-ending ripple of retribution that seemed to be foisted on her for what had once been, to her, a magical night.

But even while she hated him for the way he had been with her since he'd come back into her life, she now also understood a little better why he might possibly be acting the way he was—or, at the very least, maybe, *a part* of the reason why.

'You know him?'

Shannon laughed a bitter little laugh. 'Yeah, you could say that.'

'Who is he? Is he gay? Tell me he's gay and single and I'll love you for ever and ever.'

Connor's head turned again, his eyes searching until they eventually locked with hers. While her heart thundered in response as he then walked purposefully towards her, confidently, with determination, his dark eyes lacking in their usual hint of silent amusement.

Shannon frowned hard as she felt her body immediately react to his approach, her eyes looking down over his broad shoulders, his wide chest, all the way down his long legs. And she felt her breasts grow heavy, felt the knot forming in her abdomen.

Goddamn him! How could she hate him so much and still want him inside her so badly?

She wasn't ready to go through another confrontation. Not yet. Not while the sight of him kept on invoking such a powerful response of conflicting emotions in her. What she needed was a few more minutes to gather herself together before she spoke to him. *Just a few minutes.*

All she had to do was find a way of getting them…

'Erm, guys?' She held up her hand for silence. 'Ladies and gentlemen!'

The room fell silent and Connor hesitated, a frown darkening his face even more, if that was possible.

Shannon swept an arm in his direction. 'Mr Flanaghan is here to talk to you all. He's the new owner of Devenish Enterprises. I'm sure he won't mind answering all of your questions about the sale of the building.'

As the small crowd descended on him Mario leaned down to hiss in her ear. 'Mr Gorgeous-Hunk-O-Male is the new owner? The guy who tried to cop off with you on the dance floor before you had your big tiff?'

'He didn't try to cop off with me.' Which was an out-and-out lie, wasn't it? Would she ever stop lying?

But this one her friend wasn't buying. 'Honey, it looked like he did from where *we* were sitting. I can't begin to tell you how jealous I was of you. So, what's going on?'

'Why don't you ask *him?* He's the man of the moment.'

And with that she sneaked out of the room. The rest of the group could deal with him and vice versa while she got herself gathered together.

It took nearly a full hour before he negotiated an escape and found her upstairs.

Leaning against the doorframe, he watched in silence as she loaded dishes into cupboards, her lithe body moving fluidly as she worked her way back and forth, occasional upward stretching affording him a glimpse of smooth skin between her sweatpants and vest-top.

She had an amazing body, didn't she? Long, seemingly endless legs that ended at the perfect rounded curve of her ass, that deliciously feminine inward dip at the small of back, and as she turned a little to get to the top cupboard again he got a brief view of the flat, creamy smooth skin of her stomach and the upward lift of her pert breasts as she reached upwards.

The other night she had curved that sweet body in against his, he had felt her nipples against his chest, had had the torture of her hips moving in against his. Even while he stood in her doorway, remembering, he could feel the blood rush from his head, his groin tightening in anticipation.

He'd never wanted a woman so badly before.

And the fact that she'd said it would never happen made it an even hotter prospect in his mind—the erotic temptation of forbidden fruit.

Getting her would be a goal he could set his mind to achieving. It was something he could control at a time in his life when he needed some semblance of control. Unwittingly she had made him even more determined to get her, to torture her long and slow until she was begging him for the same kind of satisfaction he knew she'd experienced once before.

It had been a bad move in her latest game.

The reception she'd given him downstairs had been pretty much what he'd expected, barring the barrage of questions she'd forced him to face while she'd sneaked off. And in a small way he had found her method of avoidance ingenious, forcing him to smile a genuine smile of amusement on the way upstairs to see her.

Once she knew the method he'd used to get *away* from her little trap he knew he'd be smiling even more. It served her right for taking him on.

But he knew instinctively, while he stood watching her from the doorway, that she wouldn't appreciate it if he smiled a triumphant smile at her. Even if he managed not to add to his trouble with a sharp comment of some kind, many of which he had rehearsed before he'd fallen asleep the night before.

'Leaving me to the wolves was a bit sneaky, don't you think?'

The sound of his voice stiffened her spine. But, to her credit in the self-control department, she merely took a breath and continued clearing up, not even bothering to turn round to look at him.

'Nope. You're the big guy around here now. And they have a right to know why you're taking this place from them. On your head be it, Mr Big-Shot.'

'It's just an old building like plenty of other old buildings in this city—it's outlived its usefulness to the company. It's nothing personal. I believe I've mentioned that a time or two already.'

'Well, I'm willing to bet they didn't see it that way when you talked to them downstairs.'

She was right, they hadn't. Truthfully, Connor had been made to feel like the devil incarnate. But it *wasn't* personal, either to Shannon or the eclectic bunch of people downstairs. *And* he had promised them he would find an alternative building, same as he had with Shannon. Not that that had gone down any better with them than it had with Shannon on the day he'd arrived.

Connor just didn't get what the problem was himself. From the outside the place looked like a setting for a truly awful cheesy horror movie. And it wasn't a whole heap better inside, barring the miracles that Shannon had obviously managed with the floor she used as an apartment.

'It makes more sense to sell it when it's a saleable proposition. It's falling apart in places as it is.'

She sighed impatiently. 'Only because no one has ever bothered their backside spending any money on it.'

Connor's eyes narrowed as she slammed a cupboard door shut and turned to lean against the counter, arms crossed over her breasts as she attempted staring him out.

It was a nice try, he'd give her that. But she should know better. 'Well, do you think that could possibly be because to repair it would cost more than it would to tear it down?'

'And everything in this world comes down to money in the end, does it?'

Connor took a deep breath, glancing briefly around her apartment while he searched for patience. It wasn't by any means opulent, but she'd obviously made an attempt to make a home for herself. There was even a certain quirky charm to the place that reminded him of the Shannon he used to know. Not that he particularly wanted to be reminded of that version of her when he was intent on battling with her all the way into bed.

'I brought you brochures of new buildings to look at.'

'I already told you I don't want another building. I want this one.' Her voice remained low and calm.

Which drew his gaze back to her face—because he hadn't expected low and calm from her, not after last time. When they had both said things that couldn't be taken back.

He had been fully prepared for sarcasm and anger. And to give as good as he got.

'I told you it's already sold. It's a done deal.'

Shannon nodded. 'Because you're narrowing down the amount of properties on the company's books.'

'Exactly.'

There was a long pause while she studied his face, her long lashes blinking slowly, flickering slightly as she looked from one of his eyes to the other. Then she unfolded her arms, stretching them out to her sides and resting her hands against the wooden counter top, which allowed him to read the lettering across her breasts: '4 out of 3 people have trouble with fractions.'

And Connor felt a smile tug at the corners of his mouth again. One that grew when he noticed the rise and fall of her breasts increasing as her breathing sped up. Oh, she wasn't as cool and calm as she was pretending to be, was she?

If she was so determined not to end up horizontal with him again, then she shouldn't have such visceral reactions to him looking at her. But then if she didn't want anyone looking at her breasts she shouldn't keep wearing tops with varying different amusing sayings on them either.

She was bringing all this on herself.

When he looked up, her eyes were darker, more irritation evident in her tone when she spoke. 'So, it's not because you're trying to dismantle Devenish piece by piece?'

His smile faded. 'And why exactly would I do that?'

'You tell me.'

Shannon watched as he shook his head, his eyes narrowing a barely perceptible amount as he walked over to set the brochures he was holding onto the counter beside her. 'Let your agent know which building you're interested in and we'll get the ball rolling.'

Shannon frowned at him. 'I keep telling you I don't *want* another building, Connor. Not that you ever bother listening. But this isn't just about narrowing down properties, is it? There's more to this than that.'

'You can think what you want…' he leaned his head a little closer, his voice dropping to a low grumble '…but don't go looking for some deep psychological reason to justify why I'm selling. It's good business, that's all.'

How was she supposed to concentrate when he was so close again? He was overwhelming up close. She could see tiny paler flecks of gold in his dark eyes, could notice the small creases at the outside edges of his eyes and mouth that hinted at the constant smile he usually had close by, she could smell the scent of his expensive aftershave.

And she could hear Barry White in her head again suggesting they 'get it on'. Which was tempting—and it wouldn't take much either when he was standing so close already. In fact a tilt of her head would probably do it.

When she swiped the end of her tongue over her mouth, his intense gaze dropped, then rose, locking with hers. And for the life of her she couldn't find anything witty or sarcastic to say to him.

When he tilted his head a little past her face, she sucked in a gasp of air, holding it inside her chest while his gaze focused on the spiral of hair against her cheek. And while her heart thundered in her chest while she tried to keep her mind focused on how much she disliked him and not on how desperately she was physically attracted to him, his hand rose, trapping the end of the strand between his thumb and forefinger. But he didn't tuck it back into place, he twisted it a little so that the curl was tighter, then he let go, so that the curl bobbed briefly against her skin as his gaze went back to her mouth.

And the part of her that ached, low down inside, ignored her better judgement, so that the only thing she knew was that if he didn't kiss her soon or leave, she was going to scream.

The smile that slowly formed on his sensual mouth told her he knew what she wanted.

Shannon wanted to kill him.

She pushed her hands off the counter, attempting to move away from him, but Connor stepped in closer, pinning her in place just by standing there. Not touching, oh, no, not touching her *anywhere,* merely dominating her with his presence and the sexual static between them.

Shannon's head tilted back and she looked into his eyes with a quirk of her eyebrows.

It was apparently all the invitation he needed.

Because in a split second his hands rose, his thumbs tilting her chin up as his fingers slid back into her hair, caressing the nape of her neck as his head lowered and he grumbled above her mouth, 'You're right, though. There is more to it than that. There's this.'

Then his firm mouth settled on hers.

And it was as if a ticking time bomb went off inside her. Her hands rose, her fingers grasping the lapels of his jacket into tight fists as she vented all of her anger and frustration into the kiss. There was no tenderness to it, no gentle sense of longing. All there was was the release of the sexual tension that had been building since the day he'd walked through the foyer doors. And any need to discuss the damn building, or anything else off the long, *long* list of issues they had standing between them, left the room—at speed.

Connor's hands dropped from her face as he increased the pressure of his mouth, meeting her demands with some of his own as he plundered her lips from one edge to the other. And those hands then grasped hold of either side of her waist, pulling her forwards, grinding her pelvis in tighter against his hard body while he inhaled, drawing in the air she exhaled as she opened her mouth to give access to his tongue.

Shannon's hands rose, sliding up past his shoulders to tangle in the short, coarse hair behind his neck while she stood on her toes to demand an equal amount from the kiss. It was frantic, it was hot—everything she had fantasized about of late and so much more.

And it still damn well wasn't enough!

She gasped when he lifted her, as if she weighed nothing, depositing her on the counter so that she was slightly above him. So she was looking down at him when he wrenched his mouth free and looked up at her.

And she still couldn't speak.

He moved his hands down to her hips, down the outside of her thighs, ran his fingers under her knees and spread her legs a little wider to step between them.

And Shannon just let him.

Until his eyes searched hers, his head tilted again, and his warm breath washed over her swollen lips. 'I knew you'd be like this.'

Never in her life had there been anyone else who could wind her this tight, make her this hot this fast or force all rational thought to leave her head until there was only one thought left there.

'I've never kissed someone I didn't like before.'

He smiled, his hands moving slowly up her legs again. And the erotic suggestion of their position sent waves of moisture to Shannon's core. They could do it like this, just exactly where they were, a few less clothes, a little more kissing. It wouldn't take much.

Not when they'd been dancing around this for days.

And maybe if they just got it out of the way they could actually hold a conversation long enough to sort out a few other things.

'You liked me once. You'll learn to like me again. You've just got to allow yourself to.'

Damn it. And he'd said the words with just enough softness in his voice for her to believe him, hadn't he? While his hands stilled on her upper leg, fingers splaying so that his thumbs rested on the edge of the sensitive skin of her inner thigh.

'We were friends before we were lovers, remember, Shannon? I remember that.'

Shannon swallowed hard to shift the lump forming in her throat. Yes, they had been friends. They had laughed together, teased each other, spent time in each other's company without all this bickering and tension.

But that had been then. 'You're different now.'

He straightened a little.

But Shannon kept looking him in the eye, searching for a sign that the Connor she had known was still in there somewhere. 'And why is it you're so different, Connor?'

His hands lifted from her legs, eyes narrowing again. 'I told you not to look for some deep psychological reason behind this sale.'

'And I told you that it wasn't about the sale this time. It's not even about *this*.' She waved a hand back and forth between them.

Connor stepped back from her, his brow furrowing into a frown, his voice clipped. 'Oh, really? Then what is it about?'

It would be so much easier just to leave it, to say something to push him away and then to try her damndest never to see him again before everything got even more complicated with sex. Shannon knew that.

But she couldn't leave it be. When it came to the subject of Connor that had always been her problem, hadn't it?

So, she finally asked him in a husky voice, 'How long have you known?'

Connor's jaw tensed as he forced the question from between tight lips. 'Known what?'

'That Frank McMahon was your father.'

He stepped forwards again, his face dark with anger. *'What?'*

Shannon shimmied down off the counter so that he couldn't pin her into the same compromising situation as before, where she might get distracted from what she needed to know. 'I know, Connor. That's why you own Devenish now; he left it to you because you're his son.'

'Been doing a little investigating since the other night, haven't we?'

Shannon felt the heat build on her cheeks, 'I needed to know what I was dealing with.'

'Well, now you know.' The smile he aimed her way was anything but friendly. 'Congratulations.'

But before she could answer his sarcasm, he turned, and marched straight out of her apartment.

Leaving her standing in front of the counter with her mouth gaping open in surprise. *What?* He was just going to *leave?* He'd just wound her tight as a drum, softly reminded her of the time they used to be friends, told her she would get to like him again if she just allowed herself to—and then, when she'd given him the opening to explain why he'd been such an ass of late, he'd just *walked?*

Oh, Shannon didn't think so!

CHAPTER FOUR

SHE WAS IN THE foyer in less than a minute. From behind the reception desk, Mario glanced up, smiling knowingly before he waved a hand towards the door.

'He went that way.'

Out in the street she glanced left, then right, not noticing passing cars or anybody who wasn't Connor, until she spotted his tall frame as he held up an arm, the lights on a car slightly ahead of him flickering to signal he had opened it.

'Connor—wait a minute!'

He turned round and watched her jog down the street towards him, cautious eyes blinking slowly at her when she was standing right in front of him. While Shannon plucked the loose curl from her cheek to tuck it behind one ear before she tilted her head back.

'You're just gonna walk? You're not going to take a second to maybe talk about this?'

'There's nothing to talk about.'

Shannon laughed sarcastically. 'The hell there's not!'

She knew the anger in her voice was laced with her frustration, but she didn't try to disguise it. And for the first time since he had reappeared, she saw surprise on his face. But before she could figure out why he was surprised by it, it was swiftly replaced with yet another frown.

'Well, that's where you're wrong.'

When he turned she instinctively reached out for him, her fingers closing around the muscles of his upper arm, 'Wait damn it!'

He didn't turn to face her full on, instead glancing over his shoulder with narrowed eyes. 'Who did you speak to?'

'Tess told me.' Her hand dropped from his arm as she made the confession. 'I e-mailed her the day you got here.'

With a shake of his head, he slowly turned on his heel, towering over her as he asked, 'And you couldn't have tried something off the wall, like, I don't know, just speaking to *me* about it, like a grown-up would?'

Despite the stinging derision, Shannon laughed again. 'Oh, yeah, 'cos we've been getting on *so great,* haven't we?'

'And yet the first thing you did when I left was e-mail my sister to ask all about me.' He lowered his head a little, his dark brows rising in question. 'Where was the reasoning in that exactly?'

'What the hell else was I supposed to do?' She swung an arm out to her side. 'You just waltzed in after seven years and informed me that, not only were you some kind of millionaire, but that you're going to pull the rug out from under me as well! What did you *expect* me to do? Nothing made any sense—I needed some answers. You weren't the Connor I knew when I left and I wanted to know *why.*'

'Because the Connor you used to know couldn't possibly have made something of himself unless he won the lottery or got it handed to him on a plate?'

Shannon was astounded by his logic. '*No!* Don't be ridiculous, of course I didn't think that!'

'Why wouldn't you? It wasn't like I grew up surrounded by money, was it?'

They both knew that the Flanaghan family hadn't been wealthy growing up. Far from it. But even though Shannon had been glaringly lacking in more recent news, there were some things she had known.

'And yet you still managed to build a thriving business with Rory. One that helped support the rest of the family after your dad died. That wasn't handed to you on a platter, was it, Connor?'

It was one of the things that had made her feel the most proud of him, even after she'd left. Connor had always been so free and easy, so reluctant to take on any kind of long-term commitment, including one with a woman. Yet together with Rory he had knuckled down, shouldering real responsibility at an age when most guys were still running around acting like kids.

Connor stood tall again, his eyes searching hers for a long moment. 'Well, as it turns out, he wasn't my dad. So there you go—life's just full of surprises.' He smirked. 'Spot on with the bastard analogy, though, weren't you?'

Shannon gasped. *That* was what he had meant when he had told her she had no idea how right she was? It hadn't at all occurred to him that she had called him that because of the way he had been *behaving* at the time?

Connor's mouth twitched in response to what she knew had to be a stunned expression on her face. To a passer-by he might even have looked momentarily amused. But a passer-by wouldn't have known to search the dark depths of his eyes for that familiar silent amusement that was so often there—and noticeably absent this time. No matter how hard Shannon looked for it.

And now she was getting mad at him again. '*I* didn't *know.*

And that *wasn't* what I meant when I called you that. In case you missed it, I was *angry* at you at the time. You were being a *complete ass,* pretty much like you are now, as a matter of fact!'

He merely shrugged in answer. 'Apt, though, wasn't it?'

She watched as he took a deep breath, his gaze leaving her face and focusing at a point above her head before he nodded. 'Well. Now you know. Not that it makes any difference. I'm still selling your damn building.'

She didn't reach for him when he turned away a second time, but when he walked away she was on his heel. 'Is that why you won't take Rory's phone calls now? Why you haven't spoken to Tess? Have you spoken to *any* of them? Or are you being this much of a moron to everyone?'

'I'll speak to them when I'm ready to speak to them.'

'They're your *family.*'

Stopping at the side of his sleek car, he yanked the door open so that it acted as a barrier between them while he scowled down at her. 'Leave it alone, Shannon. It's got nothing to do with you.'

He was right. In the greater scheme of things it *didn't* have anything to do with her. It was none of her business. But apparently that didn't mean she didn't care. Because she knew how much he had to be hurting to break all contact with his family. He *had* to be.

And maybe, just maybe, that was part of the reason he was so different. She could just have a sit-down later to think about why she was still so physically attracted to him when he was so different. It certainly wasn't because she still felt anything for him.

But the part of her heart that *had* felt something once wanted to believe that that was the reason he had changed—

it didn't want to believe he had turned into someone she could hate as much as she had the last few days.

After all, the Flanaghans were the closest family she had ever known. Where one ended the other began. And Shannon knew how precious something like that was, never having had it herself. To suddenly discover that he was someone else's son must have crushed Connor. How could it not have?

When she found words again, her voice came out softer with perceived understanding. 'How long have you known?'

Dark eyes rose to the heavens for a brief second, as if searching for patience, before he sighed. 'Six weeks.'

That made it an all-too-recent wound—which gave her a glimmer of hope.

'There's no doubt about it? You spoke to your mother?'

'We had a little chat, yes.' Dark eyes locked with green. 'You done now?'

'No.' She shook her head, ignoring the curl that worked loose again to brush against her cheek. 'I don't think I am. Not if you're so keen I should allow myself to like you again.'

A heavy silence hung in the air between them while Connor's eyes studied the strand of hair against her flushed cheek. Then, just when Shannon honestly believed she would have to push yet again, his mouth curled into what looked like a half-smile, half-grimace, before he announced, 'All right, then, you want another confession, then I'll give you one. To a certain extent, you were right. When you said I was taking Devenish apart piece by piece you were pretty close to the mark. Property by property, I'm going to dump out all the original old buildings that Frank McMahon built his damn company on. I'm going to remove every hint of him from what's left and make money as I do it. Every pet project he had, every building that held sentimental value to him. I'll pull them down and build on them if I have to. So there's no way you're going to stop me from selling that place, Shannon. You need to just accept that and let it go.'

Shannon watched, wide eyed, as he lifted a hand from the top of the open door to brush the strand of hair off her cheek again, his gaze following his fingers as, this time, he tucked it neatly behind her ear.

So simple a movement, and yet there was a tenderness that hadn't been there before. A warmth in his eyes that reminded her of the Connor she had known before. And Shannon's heart twisted agonizingly inside her chest.

While his deep voice remained deathly calm as he continued carefully speaking each word with a slow, icy deliberation. 'That ugly building you care so much about is just a little part of it. No one will stop me or change my mind. Not even you, Shannon.'

Splayed fingertips resting on the sensitive skin below her ear, and on the line of her jaw, he slowly studied her face. 'But I can help you, if you'll let me. I'm an extremely rich man now. You just tell me where it is you want to move to and I'll make it happen. Then maybe we can get past this and deal with this thing that's still here between us. Because what happened in your apartment is just the beginning and you know that as well as I do.'

Shannon shook her head, the movement brushing his fingers a little deeper into her hair. 'This isn't you.'

A low grumble of laughter sounded. 'Oh, this is me, all right. Just a newer version than you're used to.'

'It's not the version of you I used to care about.'

He used his thumb to tilt her chin up. 'The version of me that you're so determined you regretted sleeping with seven years ago—is that the one you mean?'

Despite her best efforts, she felt her lower lip tremble and was forced to take a moment to bite down on it to hide the telltale sign from him. His words reminded her of the reason she had regretted it happening so much. But it was too late, and his eyes narrowed as he slipped his hand from her face, withdrawing his arm to his side.

'I guarantee you won't regret it this time. Because this time there won't be any games played. We're two adults who just happen to be extremely sexually attracted to each other. And there's only one logical conclusion to that.'

'Connor—'

'No.' He shook his head, his face an impassive mask. 'I'm not going to get into another argument with you, we're done for now.'

When she opened her mouth to protest he leaned in and silenced her with another firm, lingering kiss—taking his time with it so that she was left in no doubt that he meant what he said. Because even if he hadn't just made everything as plain as day to her with his words, the fact that her pulse jumped erratically, her breath caught, and her body immediately heated up again confirmed it.

There *could* only be the one logical conclusion.

His face mere inches from hers, he looked down into her eyes, his voice edged with calm determination.

'I have to go to a planners meeting. But I'll be back. And I'll keep coming back. You just need to get used to that. 'Cos we're not done.'

* * *

There was somewhat of a pattern forming when it came to seeing Connor when she least expected it. So, she wasn't overly surprised when he appeared during her reading of an outlandish fairy story to the small group of fascinated children two days later.

Though she *was* surprised—and possibly a tad on the miffed side—that it had taken him so long to return this time. So she frowned at him when he stopped smiling from the doorway and sat down cross-legged at the back of the room.

How was a girl supposed to do fairy and monster voices while he was sitting there?

'So you're stalking me now—is that the plan?'

It was a logical question as the last of the Yummy Mummies arrived to collect their offspring. ''Cos I should maybe warn you that there are laws against that kind of thing these days.'

'Actually, I'm not just here to see you. Even if the different voices you did were too good to have missed.' He nodded, a thoughtful expression on his face. 'I think I liked angry Mrs Bear the best.'

Shannon scowled at him. 'Why *are* you here, then?'

'Because I said I'd take some time to see what actually happens here on a day-to-day basis.'

'And *when* exactly did you say that?'

Leaning past her to lift a beanbag, he smirked at her profile. 'When you left me to the wolves that day.'

Tossing the two large cushions she had lifted onto the pile forming in one corner of the room, she took the time to wait for Connor to do the same with his beanbag, damping down the now familiar bounce of her pulse at the sight of him by concentrating on the topic of conversation.

'They talked you into spending time *here,* away from your busy, busy schedule? How did they manage that?'

It wasn't as if he'd spared time from his schedule to make good on the 'promises' he'd made to *her* the other day, when he'd left her standing in the street, more sexually frustrated than she'd ever been in her entire life. And with an ache in her chest that was refusing to go away. Even now that he was back.

'They were very persuasive. Particularly the little one—Brieda, was it? She had a walking stick?'

'Well, seeing as she was fully prepared to hit you with that very walking stick not twenty minutes before you got here, I'd say you got off lightly.' She watched with suspicion as he continued walking back and forth with her, ignoring the fact that she should be grateful it took less than half the time to clean up the room it normally did. The words 'Thank you' would have to be dragged from her lifeless body. 'What did you do to win her over, exactly?'

Connor's eyes gleamed across at her. 'I can be very persuasive myself, when I put my mind to it.'

As well she knew.

But hang on. 'You let them think that you spending some time seeing what we do here might change your mind? Wasn't that just a teeny-weeny bit of a lie?'

'I didn't say I'd change my mind, I said I'd see what you do here.' He raised his arm, throwing the last of the cushions into the corner as if he were making a basketball shot into a net. 'And the opportunity to watch some Yummy Mummy Yoga seemed too good an opportunity to miss.'

'And yet you ended up listening to a fairy story with a bunch of under fives instead.' She shook her head, avoiding looking at him while she looked round the room for something else to tidy away. 'The best-laid plans. But they do say karma will eventually come and get you one way or another. So whatever comes your way today will serve you right for getting their hopes up. You really have *no idea* what this place means to them.'

'Well, maybe I'll find out while I'm here.'

Shannon made a small snort of derision. 'No, you won't. You're on a mission. You're the man in black.' She nodded at his T-shirt, which *was* black, as it happened. 'And they're the little people you intend stomping over to get what you want. You're the baddie.'

He quirked an eyebrow at her, the silent laughter back in his eyes. 'How many of those stories have you read today?'

She rolled her eyes.

And Connor went silent while she made a meal out of putting away the last few dress-up clothes and pictures that would normally have been ignored until the next session. Still watching her, though, she could feel it, as if he were touching her. The way it always felt when he looked at her.

Shannon really hated that.

What she needed to do was find some common ground, or something they could talk about without it turning into another argument—in front of an audience. At least that way she would stand a bat's chance of getting through the day with him nearby, right?

Because if he said he was spending a day then he'd spend a day. He was too stubborn not to. Plus he got the added bonus of irritating her along the way, watching her to see if she'd accepted the fact that they were going to end up sleeping together again—which she pretty much had. It was inevitable if he kept coming back as he did.

Shannon might have known how pigheaded she could be herself, but she also knew herself well enough to know that the way things were going she would cave in to the temptation. And she'd even told herself that she could handle that. They were both adults now. They were both attracted to each other. It wasn't as if they lived in the eighteenth century. So why shouldn't she have sex with him if she wanted to?

It wasn't as if she would make the same mistake she had last time. And maybe, just maybe, it was what she needed to do to put the demons to rest…

When he spoke again, it was almost as if he read her mind. 'It'll do us good to spend some time with a crowd around us anyway—we're less likely to argue. And it might help if you spend some time around me, in company, without touching or kissing, so you get a chance to remember why it was you used to like me.'

The words raised a wry smile, even if it was a reflection of the sarcasm in her voice. 'Oh, really, and just how are we going to manage the not-arguing part? Are you gonna promise to keep your mouth shut all day? 'Cos every time either of us tries speaking it ends up in an argument of some kind, doesn't it?'

'Or doing something else we can't do in front of a crowd.' He chuckled when she glared at him. 'Maybe we just need to try and remember the time when we were friends. Pretend to be the way we used to be.'

The soft rumble of his voice in the quiet room was temptingly persuasive. But could trying to be the way they had been before really be any less dangerous than the way they were with each other in the here and now?

Shannon doubted it.

But Connor once again seemed innately able to understand

the root cause of her hesitation, even if, once again, he worded it badly. 'What's wrong—you too chicken to try? Or is it that you don't trust yourself to keep your hands off me for that long? 'Cos we could just go up to your apartment for the day and pick up where we left off if you like. You'll not hear any complaints from me. I've done nothing but think about the possibilities of that kitchen counter for two days now.'

Spinning on her heel, she glared at him across the room. 'Do you ever actually think before you open your mouth any more? Or are you just determined to torture me every chance you get?'

He smiled a very slow smile. 'You've been thinking about the possibilities too, huh?'

Her eyes narrowed in warning.

So he dropped his chin, forcing the smile off his face with some considerable effort before his brow furrowed as he looked at her from beneath thick dark lashes. 'I'm making an effort here. Doesn't that get me any Brownie points with you?'

'Oh, it takes more than that to make up for you being such an ass since you walked through those front doors.'

'You weren't exactly rolling out the welcome mat either. Sniping at each other is a two-way thing.'

With a defiant tilt of her chin, she picked up and hugged the large story book tight against her breasts. 'I didn't invite you here.'

'And when I came to Galway this time I didn't expect you to *be* here. That kind of makes us even, don't you think?'

So they stood there in the silent room for a long while, both of them staring across at the other, until Shannon honestly thought she would have been able to hear that proverbial pin drop.

Eventually she sighed in defeat. 'I give up.'

To her surprise he didn't pounce on her with another arrogant comment in answer. Instead a warm smile lit up his face, transforming him into a hypnotically charming image of the young man he used to be as he walked towards her.

'Don't ever give up, Shannon. I like the fact that you're no quitter.' He leaned in and pressed his warm mouth to her soft lips. It was a gentle kiss, an almost tender kiss, and it left her wanting so much more.

Because she didn't want gentle and tender from him. She wanted the anger and the arrogance and the sexual frustration. They were the things she could deal with.

'I thought you said no kissing?'

He grinned. 'I said not in front of a crowd.'

She shook her head in frustration.

While his grin was reined back into a smaller smile. 'In order to get through today we're *both* going to have to make a concerted effort to be nice to each other. I can do it if you can.'

She stared up at him with a look of disbelief. 'And you can still remember how to be nice?'

Still smiling, he quirked his dark brows in challenge.

So Shannon took a moment to calm herself and grumbled out, 'All right, so maybe that didn't exactly help with the making an effort to be nice.'

'Not so much.'

A forefinger waggled in his direction. 'Patronizing me won't help either.'

'Well, maybe being defensive about every single thing I say might stop you from interpreting honesty as me patronizing you. I was agreeing with you. If I bug you when I disagree with you and still manage to bug you when I agree with you, then that doesn't leave us much to work with, does it?'

Hell. He was right, wasn't he? It was just that hating him and wanting him and the conflict of the two emotions were so much safer for her. If she started to *like* him again…

Frowning at the thought, she watched with cautious eyes as he reached for her face, his smile still in place as he cupped her cheek. And every part of her instinctively wanted to either turn tail and run or to stand and fight. It was a basic animal instinct, she supposed. When confronted by something considered to be predatory, or just plain old dangerous to one's well-being.

At least Barry White had stopped singing in her head. Though that was probably because she'd started to *listen* to what he was saying.

Clearing her throat, she looked Connor straight in the eye. 'If any single one of those people out there asks me directly if I think you'll change your mind about this place, I won't lie. You need to know that. They're relying on me to find a solution to this. You're the enemy. I shouldn't even be fraternizing with you as far as they're concerned. And I'm not entirely sure I disagree with them on that one.'

And then she went silent.

Connor studied her face for a while. 'You're still trying to weigh up whether or not it's worth the effort being nice to me, aren't you? It better not be because you're toying with the idea somewhere inside that head of yours that you'll manage to change my mind by *being* nice?'

Damn it! How could he *know* that? It was something that had only just crossed her mind! Though, realistically, it would be a much more difficult plan to follow through on…

'Much as I love this place, and the people in it, there's a limit to just how "nice" I'd be to get you to change your mind. If that's what you're asking me.'

The low rumble of deep male laughter caught her completely off guard. So that she was once again temporarily mesmerized, this time by the sound as it echoed around the high ceilinged room.

Before he answered in a husky tone, 'If I was the kind of man that felt he had to blackmail a woman into being "nice" to him, I might take that offer a little further…'

Shannon's mouth opened in outrage.

But Connor held a hand up, palm towards her, before she could rise to the bait. 'But I'm not. Nothing you do would change my mind.'

'Well, then, there's not much point in—'

He leaned his head down towards her face. '*But*—I thought about it some and it seemed understanding this place was the right thing to do—and not just because the place means so much to you. It obviously means something to the wolves as well.'

'It might have made more sense to understand *before* you made your decision in the first place.'

'Maybe.'

Really? Shannon's eyes widened in surprise. *Wow.* He'd just backed down an inch there, hadn't he?

She swallowed before asking, forcing down another sarcastic reply, 'What is it you really want Connor?'

He smiled again.

While she quirked an arched brow in question.

Which gained her a smile that made it all the way up into his eyes, 'I take it you're not looking at me to give you the obvious answer to that?'

She quirked her eyebrow again.

And he chuckled. 'That's what I thought. All right, then,

maybe the idea of a day off appealed to me too—two birds and one stone and all that.'

Shannon suddenly thought about what his life must be like in the here and now. It was funny it had never occurred to her before. Any time he had 'popped by' it had been a fleeting visit between meetings, he'd always been dressed in a suit, apart from that one night in the bar, when he'd been drinking alone and more than likely seeking 'company'.

And he'd broken all contact with his family, maybe even his friends as well…

Didn't he ever get lonely while he was on his 'mission'? Not that she doubted for a second he'd ever be short of female company—she'd seen firsthand the way women had reacted to him in the bar that night…

But had he gotten so obsessed with what he was doing that he hadn't taken the time to remember what it was like to be around people, *real* people, who laughed and talked and forgot their troubles for a while?

And suddenly the idea of him spending time in the building, surrounded by the eclectic family she loved, didn't seem so bad an idea. If he had anything resembling a heart left, then surely he would soften to them as the day went on? And then Shannon could maybe butter him up a little bit more later on…

'Pulling the world apart at the seams taking it out of you is it?'

The lack of sarcasm in her tone, accompanied with a teasing light in her eyes, was enough to keep the smile on his face. 'It *can* be a little draining, as it happens.'

'I'd imagine so—' she tried an answering smile on for size '—but then they do say life's what we make it…'

'Not always. Sometimes life is what someone else made for us and we don't get a big choice in it.'

It was the first real insight into how he was really feeling that Shannon had been given. And was the first thing to allow her to let go a little, to be more relaxed—and to say what she thought.

'Do you really think he left you Devenish to make you miserable? I doubt that was what he had in mind at the time.'

The warmth in Connor's eyes faded. 'You knew him that well, did you?'

'No, I never met him.'

'Then you can't know what he was thinking. From where I stand it would have been much better if he'd left it the hell alone.'

Any warmth in his voice that had been there before was rapidly disappearing, and Shannon sensed that she was in danger of losing her window of opportunity.

Think, woman, think!

A surprisingly big part of her wasn't willing to let go of the small chance to do some good—make him realize there was a life beyond his vendetta, show him the damage he would do with the sale of the building, maybe even in some small way compensate for what she had done so many years ago by giving him a chance to get a life for himself again.

So, she took a breath and allowed her thoughts to stray into an area that she had tried to avoid as much as humanly possible.

'Would you have been able to leave it alone if you'd had a son out there somewhere?'

For the longest while he studied her eyes so intently that she feared he might see into her mind again.

But then he simply took a breath, his deep voice firm and determined. 'I'd not have waited until I was dead to do something for him. I'd search to the end of the earth for a child of mine. And he'd grow up knowing his father and where he came from.'

The words were like a knife in Shannon's heart.

When she didn't speak, Connor continued to stare deep into her eyes. 'I can't forgive him for not doing that, any more than I can forgive my mother for not telling me sooner. It just goes to prove that a lie on top of a lie doesn't ever have a good outcome.'

And still she couldn't find words.

Which brought a smile back to the sensual curve of his mouth. 'And now that you've pried that out, can we agree to try and be nice for the day? Because that happens to be the most discussion I've had on the subject.'

Shannon knew that, without even having to search his eyes for confirmation. Connor had shut himself off while he took revenge on the father he had never known. It was his way of working through it. Maybe not the right way, or the way she would have chosen herself, but it was the path he had taken.

Did that mean that the Connor she had known was still in there? Did it mean that he hadn't actually changed into someone she could hate as much as she had once loved him?

Shannon swiped the end of her tongue over her dry lips, pursing them together while she avoided his searching gaze. 'Maybe you needed to talk about this more than you thought you did.'

'Maybe.' He nodded in agreement. 'And maybe we didn't stand a chance at any kind of a temporary peace treaty until I told you even that much. I'm told trust is a two-way street.'

'I'd heard that.'

Mimicking her earlier move, he tilted his head to bring his face back into her line of vision, waiting until her long lashes rose and she was looking him in the eye again. 'So, what do you do after the story-telling, then? You're gonna have to keep me busy if I'm going to stick to the no kissing or touching rule.'

The silence was suddenly broken by the echo of music from the next room.

Connor's brows rose in surprise, his head turning to seek out the source of the sound. 'What's that?'

'They run a dance class here on a Friday. Jive, ballroom, that kind of thing.' She listened for a moment until the track was familiar to her. 'Sixties today, by the sound of it, so it'll be jive. All age groups can do that in varying degrees.'

When he looked back at her his dark eyes were lit up with what she immediately recognized as devilment. 'Excellent.'

'What are you doing?'

He had hold of her hand again. 'You want to show me what goes on here—then let's go. Dancing is close enough to the touching thing to keep me happy.'

'O-h-h no.' Her laughter was a little more genuine this time. 'I think we've established that when we dance together it isn't just dancing—it's foreplay.'

The tugging stopped while he smiled down at her with the kind of gorgeously sexy smile that set her alight every single time. 'I can behave if you can. And anyway—' he leaned closer to whisper in her ear '—play your cards right and the whole day will be like foreplay.'

Shannon shook her head. 'If your ego gets any bigger you'll have to give it a name of its own.'

Connor chuckled. 'It's either dancing or we go re-enact that scene from the movie in the Potty about Pottery class later. Your choice. I'm here to experience it all.'

A very vivid image of them sitting at a pottery wheel while

wet clay slid between their joined fingers did things to Shannon's pulse rate that she was quite sure shouldn't happen without her needing a heart monitor—and suddenly dancing seemed the safer option. So, setting the large book on a small chair beside them, she took a deep breath and tightened her fingers around his.

'You're just gonna love the embroidery class.' With her hand still holding tightly to his, she pulled him towards the door. 'Of course, then there's Tumblin' Tinies at six on this floor, a meditation class at seven, and—'

Connor squeezed her hand as they walked into the foyer and made the turn into the next room. 'Persuading me this place is so damn great might go better if you didn't make it all sound like some kind of endurance test.'

With her hand pushing the door open, she looked back at him with gleaming eyes, a bubble of mischief forming in her chest. Well, it was either that or nervous energy.

'I remember you having more of a sense of adventure, Connor Flanaghan.'

Connor merely grinned in response, raising his other hand to the small of her back to guide her forwards. 'Attempting to jive with a woman dressed as a fairy-tale princess is adventurous enough for me for one day.'

Shannon's chin dropped, her mouth an 'o' of surprise as she suddenly remembered what she was wearing. In a way she should have been thankful that he hadn't visited last week when she'd been dressed as a leprechaun, but even so…

'I can't jive in this!'

'Sure you can. If you can dance dressed as an Egyptian dancing girl then this should be a cinch.' He ignored the look of shocked outrage on her face at the mention of her seduction apparel from back in the day. 'Though I sincerely hope you kept that all these years. I wasn't done with it when you left in the middle of the night.'

Before Shannon could make a comment, he looked over her head and smiled in greeting—so she had to make do with smiling at the class as they joined it while swallowing down another sharp shard of pain in her chest.

Then she sent up a silent plea that she hadn't just got in over her head…

Again.

CHAPTER FIVE

'ALL RIGHT, WHAT'S next?'

Connor leaned across the counter in an attempt to read Shannon's diary upside down, glancing up at her face to see what he could see in her eyes while silently hoping there wasn't anything else in the damn diary. He knew what activity he wanted to spend the rest of the evening doing.

And it didn't involve a crowd.

The day had certainly brought a great deal more enjoyment than he had thought it would, even if he did now have more information on embroidery and pottery than he would ever be likely to use in everyday life. He'd obviously needed a break more than he had realized if playing around with bunches of kids, unemployed teenagers and old-age pensioners had brought a smile to his face.

But he knew it had more to do with being with Shannon. Because he'd been right—the day *had* turned into a kind of slow foreplay. Surrounded by people the entire time, each brief touch or sideways glance had felt as if it were stolen, forbidden somehow, which made it unbelievably erotic.

So that he had ended up having to focus on each new

activity with increasing degrees of attention in order to keep his mind off whisking her away for more adult activities.

It had been hard. *Literally.*

But there was something new between them too, something invisible that started as a niggle and became a nagging voice in his mind as the day progressed. And the fact that he couldn't put a finger on what it was was becoming more and more of a source of irritation to him.

It distracted him from the crackling sensual awareness that had been there all day, which at times had probably been useful, but Connor wasn't sure he wanted to be distracted from that *now.*

Which meant he was going to have to risk life and limb by trying to find out what it was, didn't it?

But it was bugging him.

She glanced up at him with a small smile, then back down at the diary. 'Oh, I think what you've done already could be deemed going above and beyond the call of duty. I was kidding when I said you had to do everything.'

Above and beyond the call of duty, maybe, but at least now he understood what happened there every day. They ran an eclectic group of activities to go with the equally eclectic group of people that came through the doors. But he still didn't get why it was the location made that big a difference…

'You wouldn't be trying to get rid of me, would you, Sunshine?'

She tried to hide it, but he caught sight of another small smile twitching at the edges of her mouth before she forced it away. It was something she'd been doing a lot of in the last hour or so. Almost as if she was giving away too much ground by showing she was having fun.

Though she hadn't managed to hide those smiles any better than she had the heated gazes they had exchanged.

Her long lashes flickered as she glanced up at his face again, green eyes studying him for a long moment while he smiled back at her.

Then she sighed, closing the diary. 'There's only film night left. And it's not for another half hour.'

'What's film night?'

Her head tilted, arched eyebrows rising in amused disbelief.

And Connor chuckled in response. 'What *kind* of film? 'Cos I don't do chick flicks. And why don't they just go to a cinema like other people do?'

'A lot of them like to come to somewhere close to home 'cos they find getting around tough as they've gotten older. And it's not a *chick flick;* it's a black and white movie night. We do all the classics—anything I can get on DVD anyway. You'll hate it. No blowing up things, no naked women, no fast cars.'

'You don't know I won't like it.'

'You'll be happy watching some period melodrama from the forties with a bunch of over seventies?'

He blinked at her. 'You said it *wasn't* a chick flick.'

'Not the way *you'd* think of one. But it's still hardly going to be anywhere near butch enough for you.'

Well, flattering and all as it was she thought him butch, she was right. A black and white movie wouldn't be his usual choice of activity for a Friday night. But after the twenty minutes he'd managed in the meditation class before laughing he reckoned he could pretty much endure anything she threw his way. It had become some kind of test in her eyes and he knew it. Which only made him want to succeed all the more at the things she'd decided he would fail at—so he shrugged.

'Depends on how good the film is, and whether you can manage to rustle us up some popcorn and a seat on the back row.'

Shannon studied him in silence.

'You don't *want* me to stay is the truth. You didn't think I'd last this long, even when you should know me better. And it kills you to admit you've had fun with me being here.'

'This wasn't supposed to be about me having fun, it was supposed to be about you understanding what we have going here.'

What they had 'going' remained to be seen in Connor's eyes. Occasionally, just very occasionally during the day, there would be small flashes of the way they used to be when they were together. Honest to goodness laughter, silly teasing comments, mutual understanding of a wisecrack that others around them might not necessarily have got.

It was exactly what he'd been missing of late. Just spending time in someone's company doing things that weren't a constant reminder of how complicated his life had become or the associated permanent bad mood that accompanied it was like taking a holiday.

But there was more simmering beneath the surface too—an anticipation of what was to come. He'd known it from the moment he had mentioned the 'disguise' she'd worn that one time, and the green of her eyes had darkened a shade. And he had felt it when they had danced again, when her body had moved with his and she would quietly catch her breath, or when he would spin her away and back and her breathing would speed up as she'd looked at him with languid eyes.

Every move, all day, had been a precursor.

He took a breath, his gaze still locked on hers as he smiled. 'You're not getting rid of me, you know. You're stuck with me.'

And there was the something again.

His smile remained. 'There's that look again. Do you want to tell me exactly what it is I've inadvertently done to bug you *this* time?'

'I don't know what you mean.' She made a show of straightening some of the papers laid out on the wide counter top, her hand moving up briefly to brush the corkscrew curl back into place.

Which made him smile again. She'd always done that thing with her hair when she was nervous, from way back when she was young. The mass of soft curls had been tough to control at the best of times, and Shannon had been so damn determined to tame it. As if she had to be in control of everything, or that it working loose from whatever band she had it in was a sign of her quirky personality trying to escape from the restraints she had on it.

A quirkiness she had no problem exhibiting these days. *Oh, no*. Her latest T-shirt announced: 'My imaginary friend thinks you have serious mental problems.'

'You do that when you're nervous, you know.' He nodded his head at the curl, which bobbed loose the minute she looked up at him. 'You always did.'

Her hand rose, stilled, and went back down to the counter while she mumbled back, 'Yes, well, I keep thinking I should just get it cut. But I never do.'

'I'm glad.'

She cleared her throat. 'Look, I normally don't stay down here for the film nights anyway—'

The gregarious, over-the-top Mario chose that moment to bound down the stairs beside the reception area with a large box of buttered popcorn in bags. 'I have the chairs all in place and the DVD wired up to the screen. Just the popcorn to put out and the tea urn to fill and that's me. I've saved your usual place near the back so that no one tries to steal it this time.'

He winked at Connor on the way past, 'Can't have some wrinkly taking her place, now, can we? She loves these things. Never misses a weepy, does our Shannon.'

Connor smiled, nodding at Shannon as Mario disappeared into the room that had been used earlier for the kids' story time session. 'Normally don't stay down for these, huh?'

A pink tinge was working its way up her neck. 'I don't go to every single one.'

'Yeah, I got that from the words "never misses".'

She sighed, her shoulders dropping. 'Look, Connor, I've been watching you today and it's pretty plain you think it's all some big joke here. Watching an old film with a room full of pensioners is hardly going to change your opinion, so why don't you just go do whatever it is you normally do on a Friday night while I try and find a way of breaking it to them all that there's nothing they can do to change your mind?'

When she turned to walk out from behind the counter, Connor pushed up off his elbows and stepped around, blocking her exit. 'Actually, you're wrong—I do understand a bit better what goes on here. It'll help me to find a replacement building that's right for everyone.' He dipped his head down to look up into her eyes. 'You're sure there's not something else bugging you? I thought as the day went on, if nothing else, we were making some headway towards remembering how to get along again.'

'There's not much point in us getting along.'

'I disagree.'

'There's a surprise.'

He stepped a step closer. 'There were plenty of times today when you looked happy I was here. And plenty of times when you looked at me with the same thing on your mind that I had.'

Shannon tried a sidestep and was blocked. 'Well, there were times when watching you trying to join in with some of the activities was amusing to watch, I'll give you that.'

Another forward step. 'I had fun, surprisingly—though I doubt I'll be taking up any of the activities in the near future. Go on, now you try—"I had fun too Connor. I'm glad you were here." You can even tell me how impressed you were with that gorgeous pot I made in the pottery class.'

She flashed him a brief smile. They both knew the pot had been horrifically sad. Then she stilled, her mouth pursed into a thin line while she studied the collar of his shirt. 'All right, I will admit there may have been *moments* of fun in there that reminded me of how you used to be.'

'For me too.'

The soft words brought her gaze up again, her throat convulsing as she swallowed, and Connor's eyes were inexorably drawn down to the rise and fall of her breasts, the movement speeding up the longer he looked, until eventually he forced his gaze upwards to lock with hers.

She glanced around the room, then back into his eyes, a smile teasing her full mouth again. 'Stop that.'

He smiled at the slightly breathless demand. 'Stop what?'

'You know rightly what.' The tone of her voice took on a huskier edge. 'You have a way of looking at a woman when you want her that leaves her in no doubt about what you're thinking. And that's a tad inappropriate in company. You'll give me a bad name.'

'Is that why your mood changed during the Tumblin' Tinies session?'

'My mood didn't change.'

'Yeah, it did. You looked at me at one point like I'd just taken the thing you loved the most from you and tossed it over my shoulder.'

The *something* was there again as her hand rose to fiddle the curl back into place, her eyes avoiding his. 'Which, believe it or not, you *are* by selling this place. I guess I just foolishly allowed myself to believe for a while that being here might help you understand that.'

Connor's smile faded, because his gut was telling him there was more to it than that, even if her answer did make sense *to her*. And he hated that she felt the need to lie to him. There'd been more than enough of that in his life lately. But, frankly, despite the warm atmosphere within the crumbling walls, he still didn't get what the attachment was.

'I've made it plain from the start I wouldn't change my mind, Shannon. So how come it only hit you while I helped with those kids? 'Cos that was when you first had that look you're wearing now. Is there something else you want to tell me?'

'No, there's nothing else I want to tell you!' Her eyes flashed when she looked back into his. 'Maybe for a little while I *did* manage to convince myself that you being around these people might change your mind. The more time you've spent here smiling and having fun, the more I've seen the hope come back onto people's faces—and that has *killed me*. Because today isn't about fun or friendship, it's just business to you—a deal you made to get out of any explanations the other day. This is "nothing personal"—isn't that the phrase you like the most?'

Ignoring the sneer that accompanied her words, Connor stepped closer again, so that his body was almost touching hers, the minute distance between them seeming to spark with tension again. Then he waited, studying her flashing green eyes, the slight flare of her nostrils as she took shuddering breaths, and he knew, deep down in his gut, that she was still lying to him.

'I think you know why I spent an entire day here—and it had nothing to do with business and everything to do with something personal. It's not about the building. This is about you and me.'

'It's not just about you and me, Connor. How can you not know that? How can I have sex—'

Connor silenced her with a single long finger against her lips, smiling when she froze and looked up at him with wide, angry eyes. 'Shush a minute.'

The eyes narrowed.

'We've done pretty damn well to go nearly a whole day without yet another big bust up, so let's try a little longer, shall we?'

Her head tilted to one side.

Connor nodded. 'Yes, I know you don't think that you're the only one causing the argument, but this time I can say with a good measure of "smug" thrown in that *I* didn't start this one.'

The lips beneath his finger parted slightly.

'You're only trying to argue with me because there's something else that you don't want to talk about. And I get that. Because that's the kind of thing *I* normally do.'

There was a small puff of air against his finger as she exhaled.

'We're not all that different, you and me. And if you remember, we used to argue a lot back in the day—only you liked to call them "debates." This is nothing new with us; it's just a new topic.'

In the brief silence, her eyes softened a shade and Connor knew he was making progress.

'The only difference between then and now, Shannon, is we don't know each other as well as we used to. You've probably got as much baggage from the last seven years as I have.'

And there was that 'something' again. Briefer this time, but there long enough for him to see it while he was studying her so up close. What was it? *He'd* be lying if he told himself he didn't want to know.

But, truth be told, Connor was getting tired of arguing over the damn building. It was getting in the way.

'I'll have a think about what it is that makes this building so important, all right? I still mightn't change my mind, but I'll think about it.'

This time her quirked eyebrows told him she didn't believe him.

So he smiled. 'Don't push your luck. That's a concession and you know it is.'

'Maybe I do.' The softly spoken, reluctant words moved her lips against his finger almost like a kiss.

He turned his hand so that he was cupping her chin and still had a finger brushing against her bottom lip, back and forth, back and forth; the softness of her mouth fascinating him out of speech while he suddenly became more aware of the familiar flowery scent that had only drifted occasionally by him during the day.

'Connor—'

She said his name softly. In a way that could be interpreted as a plea for him to stop or a need for him to take what he was doing a step further. And considering how she had looked at him for a good portion of the day he decided to believe it was the latter.

And there wasn't anyone around to make it a break in the rules…

So, with his gaze still fixed on her mouth, he lowered his head and pressed an almost exploratory kiss there. Which she didn't fight him on, so he took it as an invitation to continue, his mouth becoming firmer on hers, searching from edge to edge.

But just when it was occurring to him that, unlike any of the other times he had kissed her, this time *he* was the only one doing the kissing—there was the creak of the door behind them and a stunned gasp of outrage.

Lifting his mouth from hers he looked down into her wide eyes just before she tilted her head to look over his shoulder.

'Hello, Brieda, Connie. Early as usual, I see. Mario has pretty much everything ready.'

Connor stifled his laughter before turning round to face the twin looks of disapproval on the older women's faces. 'Ladies.'

The smaller of the two made remarkably quick progress across the foyer to them, leaning heavily on her walking stick. '*Mr* Flanaghan. When we said you should see what was on offer here we weren't referring to Shannon.'

'Brieda—'

Connor smiled down at her. 'No, now we can't have Brieda thinking I go around kissing women all over the place, can we?'

The little woman harrumphed at him. 'And don't you?'

All right, she maybe had a point there. He was no angel, after all. But this was different. 'I've known Shannon a long time. From way before I owned this place.'

The announcement seemed to knock some of the wind

out of her sails, momentarily. 'Well, then, why are you selling her home?'

When he glanced sideways at Shannon she had her arms folded across her chest and a look of challenge on her face. He wasn't getting any help from there.

'We're still discussing that one, as it happens.'

'Are you indeed?'

There was just something about being 'told off' by a woman of Brieda's age that made a man remember being scolded as a child, and the thought made Connor smile all the more. But it didn't have quite the same effect on Brieda that it normally had on the female gender.

She simply scowled even harder at him.

So he tried some charm instead, wrapping an arm around Shannon's shoulders to draw her close to his side as he tilted his head and announced with a nod of his head. 'We were sweethearts.'

Shannon gasped beside him, her head leaning back a little so she could stare up at him in shock. 'Oh, we *so* were not, you big liar!'

With deliberate slowness, he lowered his chin to ask in a low voice, 'And how exactly would you like to describe to the nice lady the way we were?'

The flush on her cheeks was immediate, the flash of anger in her eyes swift to follow. And Connor felt his mouth twitch with amusement even though he knew that laughing would put him straight back into hot water again. '*Well?* Please feel free to put it into your own words.'

After another brief narrowing of her eyes, she returned her gaze to Brieda. 'It was a long time ago.'

'Did he break your heart?'

Connor shook his head, still silently amused that no matter what was said he was still the 'baddie.' 'No, actually, *she* left *me.*'

'I did not *leave you!*'

'You didn't speak to me before you got on a plane and disappeared for seven years—it *sounds* like you leaving to me. What do you think, Brieda?'

The answer was mulled over for a while. 'Well, it certainly sounds like she left. But you must have done something. Did he do something?'

Connor turned to watch the play of emotions over Shannon's face, the colour in her cheeks increasing while she tried to think of an answer. 'Well, it was kind of…complicated. And I had already planned to leave before—'

Connor grinned when her gaze flew to meet his.

Which she answered with a glare before focusing back on Brieda. 'Before we…' she tilted her head sideways in emphasis '*…got together.*'

Connor dropped his chin, shaking his head as he spoke. 'And she never wrote me a letter or left a forwarding address or an e-mail…'

When he glanced at her from the corner of his eye, another glare headed his way. 'Your sister had my e-mail address if you wanted to talk to me so bad—which you obviously *didn't.*'

'Well, you see, that's the difference between being twenty-four and thirty-one. At twenty-four I hadn't been given any encouragement to go after what I wanted. At thirty-one I know enough about what I do and don't want to pursue what I do until I get it.'

Shannon gaped at him. And when he looked at Brieda she was staring at him through narrowed eyes. So he decided to quit while he was ahead.

'Well, I have to say, I'm really looking forward to this film, ladies. How long 'til it starts?'

Shannon shook her head, as if she was clearing her thoughts to think about the answer. 'Erm, half an hour give or take.'

'Okay, then. I'll be right back.' With what he meant as a winning smile aimed at the older women, he winked at Shannon before coming out from behind the counter. 'Save a seat for me.'

CHAPTER SIX

THE FILM TITLES were rolling by the time Connor came back.

And sitting in her usual place at the back of the room, Shannon had been glad of the break so that she had some time to think. In order to make sense of all the things he had said, all the looks he had given her during the day, and all of the varying emotions she was currently experiencing that went with them.

She didn't need this again. Really she didn't.

There had been times during the day when he had been exactly the Connor she had once been head over heels over. And that was just plain old playing *dirty!*

The creak of the door heralded his arrival and was swiftly followed by a set of reproving tuts and sighs while he found his way to her side. Where there was a space on the large worn sofa against the back wall.

And she had *tried* to quietly get rid of that space, had even threatened Mario that she would fire him if *he* didn't sit there. But all her 'friend' had done was grin, inform her he was *a volunteer* and therefore couldn't be fired, wink, and then add that if he were her he'd have paid him to stay away.

So she sighed in resignation as the sofa dipped under

Connor's weight while he leaned close to hiss, 'Did I miss anything exciting?'

'The titles.'

'So what's it called?'

'Brief Encounter.'

She glanced at his profile as he looked at the large screen the film was playing on. 'I thought you said this *wasn't* a chick flick.'

'It's a *classic.*'

'A classic *chick flick?*'

'Seriously—don't you have *anything* better to do on a Friday night but bug me?'

'Not this Friday night, I don't.'

Shannon sighed again. It was just too damn exhausting to keep up with this constant game they were playing. For ever trying to stay one step ahead, to play it by her own rules instead of his while trying to ignore the constant physical ache for him and trying to be patient and give him a chance to redeem himself on the building issue. She needed a rest from it, even if it was just for the length of a film.

There was a rustling sound from next to her, 'Hold out your hand.'

'What for?'

'Just hold out your hand.'

'I'm not closing my eyes for a *surprise.*'

His tone remained calm, but Shannon was sure she could detect the familiar note of humour laced through it. 'I didn't ask you to close your eyes. *Yet.*'

The rustling came again, so Shannon leaned forwards a little to see if she could find out what it was. Only to have Connor warn, 'No peeking. *Hand.*'

The Reader Service™ — Here's how it works:

Accepting your free books places you under no obligation to buy anything. You may keep the books and gift and return the despatch note marked "cancel." If we do not hear from you, about a month later we'll send you 6 brand new books and invoice you just £2.89* each. That's the complete price — there is no extra charge for postage and packing. You may cancel at any time, otherwise every month we'll send you 6 more books, which you may either purchase or return to us — the choice is yours.

*Terms and prices subject to change without notice.

If offer card is missing write to: The Reader Service, PO Box 676, Richmond, TW9 1WU

THE READER SERVICE™
FREE BOOK OFFER
FREEPOST CN81
CROYDON
CR9 3WZ

NO STAMP
NECESSARY
IF POSTED IN
THE U.K. OR N.I.

She pursed her lips together while she considered disobeying him. Because it had damn well *been* an order, hadn't it? But for the sake of a quiet life she held out her hand, palm upwards.

Warm fingers cupped in underneath it—more rustling, and then something was set onto her palm with his other hand.

She squinted to see what it was. 'What is it?'

'Put it in your mouth and see.'

'I bet you say that to all the girls.'

His bark of laughter earned several turning heads and a 'shh' from near the front, so he leaned closer to her to whisper, 'Just try it.'

With caution she lifted it from her hand, sniffing it for good measure before she popped it in her mouth, her eyes widening as the flavour spread out to tickle her taste buds into response. And she immediately turned her face towards his to whisper, 'You brought *Dolly Mixtures?*'

'Mmm-hmm.'

There was more rustling and Shannon watched in wonder as he popped a sweet into his mouth, the scent of candy immediately invading the air between them. It also meant that, when he whispered again, it was while still chewing. 'I'll pick out the jelly ones for you. You can thank me later.'

Shannon couldn't help but smile at him. Even the fact that he had remembered what she liked from back in the day warming a part of her heart that she had forgotten.

'How can you possibly remember to do that you moron?' She never had been able to stand the coconut taste of the other sweets.

'I have the memory of an elephant.' He leaned in close again. 'Another one?'

A nod of her head accompanied with an outstretched palm earned her a glint of white teeth in the dim light. After another rustle of the paper bag, his fingertips grazed against her palm and she smiled all the more.

Connor settled back deeper into the sofa with a deep sigh. 'I've decided to win you over with charm. My good looks and bulging wallet aren't having the usual effect.'

Shannon laughed quietly. 'Charm, huh?'

'Yup.' He leaned in a little closer. 'How am I doing?'

Not too shabby, as it happened. *Damn it.*

When she didn't answer he announced in a slightly louder whisper, 'Anyway, you can't watch a film without Dolly Mixtures. It's illegal.'

'You're a five-year-old in disguise, aren't you?'

'Nah.' The answer was whispered intentionally slowly. 'I'm a big boy now.'

The innuendo made her laugh again. The combination of being too tired to keep taking umbrage at everything he said, accompanied by a sudden sense of less complicated times between them, served to lull her into what was most likely a false sense of momentary security.

But he was truly incorrigible.

'How big a bag did you get?' She tried again to peer over his large frame only to have him lift both hands to her shoulders to pull her back beside him as he leaned deeper into the cushions, so she ended up shoulder to shoulder, arm to arm, hip to hip and thigh to thigh with him.

And she almost moaned aloud with the immediate reactions in her body. How in hell had she come to be such a walking set of raging hormones of late?

Connor turned a little so that her shoulder was against his chest, one long arm arcing upwards, then curling around her shoulders so that she was held close.

'What are you doing?'

'Another film tradition when sitting on the back row. And if you don't stay put and stop chattering in my ear there'll be no more sweets—I'll eat them all. I haven't been fed dinner yet.'

After a brief inner debate, she softened a little, settling against him as he handed her another sweet. But she couldn't relax, couldn't turn off her mind any easier than she could stop herself from being aware of everywhere he touched, or aching everywhere he *wasn't* touching.

He was making her insane. Okay, that ship had probably sailed—*more* insane would be more accurate.

But already she was beginning to wonder if she could cope with sex for sex's sake with him. All day he had been reminding her of the past, when he had been the young man she had silently loved. He'd been warm and funny and attentive and charming and hot as hell to look at all day long—and now he'd popped out and bought her favourite sweets.

It really wasn't fair. *Damn him!*

By sitting watching a film and being handed her favourite jelly sweets from her teenage years she wasn't forgetting any of the bigger issues, no way. Because she had told the truth when she'd said it had killed her to see hope on the faces of the people she cared about.

And now she was just so conflicted!

The movie continued, the palm of her hand brushed by Connor's fingertips at regular intervals. And her mind meandered to when he had said that she had 'left him,' suggesting there had been more to their relationship than friendship and a one-night stand—which there hadn't been.

No matter how much she had wished there had been at the time…

Right now, a big part of her really just wished he'd go away—far away from her sight and her physical proximity—so that she could *think* clearly.

'So, what is this movie about exactly?'

Shannon rolled her eyes. 'You are such a Neanderthal. It's *Brief Encounter*—it's famous.'

She felt his shoulder shrug beside her. 'Still don't get what it's about and I've been watching ten minutes now. You'll have to enlighten me.'

'You are really going to suck as a millionaire, you know, if you can't appreciate the finer things in life like all-time classic movies, fine wine, the opera…'

'Nah, I'm perfect millionaire material. I was training to be a playboy before I even had money.'

Shannon squirmed round a little to look at his profile in the dim light. 'You see, that's another one of those statements that keeps reminding me that I don't know you any more. Give me one good reason why I should bother getting involved with you again.'

Connor shrugged. ’Cos you already are.'

Damn again. He had her on that one.

'And do you like who you are now? Won't you worry that people will only be nice to you *because* you're a millionaire and they think they'll have something to gain?'

She raised her palm again, waiting patiently while the rustling signalled Connor's search for another sweet. When he found it and leaned forward to set it into her hand, his fingers lingered there, brushing softly against her skin.

'Shannon Hennessey, are you trying to pick a fight with me again?'

'No, I'm trying to hold a conversation with you.'

His face turned towards hers, hidden in shadows as his fingertips stilled, his voice so low she had to lean forwards to hear him. 'It just kills you that you're still attracted to me, doesn't it?'

She scowled at him. But it was pointless. No matter how she tried, she couldn't see his face properly in the dark, so there was no way he could see hers.

But apparently he could see better than she thought he could, because when his fingers left her palm he reached up and tucked her lock of hair in place without faltering, the scent of the sweets stronger again as his breath washed over her face. One finger traced down the side of her face, along the fine line of her jaw—hand turning, his knuckles brushing her cheek, finding her mouth, moving back and forth in gentle strokes.

Dear Lord. Would this sweet agony never end?

'In answer to your question—' his whispered words sounded close to her ear '—no, I don't worry that people will just be nice to me because I have money. Money gets respect, that's all.'

Hypnotized by his warm touch against her face, Shannon had to take a moment to concentrate on what he was saying. If nothing else to try and stop from ending up kissing him on the sofa at the back of a room full of pensioners—ones that wouldn't approve of who she was kissing.

'It doesn't buy happiness, though.'

'No. It doesn't.' And the deep tone of his voice told Shannon that he knew that only too well.

How many people would sell their souls for the kind of money Connor had had handed to him? But it really *hadn't* brought him happiness, had it? In fact, if anything, it had so far probably brought him the exact opposite.

She just couldn't believe that had been Frank McMahon's intention. He'd probably been trying to right a wrong somehow.

While she mulled that over, Connor's fingers sliding down the column of her neck, her gaze moved around the room to see who might be watching, settling on an elderly couple near the front just as the man reached his arm over the woman's shoulder.

And she smiled at the sight, reaching up to tangle her fingers with Connor's before setting their joined hands in her lap. Then she turned a little towards him, her chin tilting up as she sought his eyes in the dim light. 'Can you see the couple in the front on the right?'

Connor turned his face to look, leaving Shannon focusing on his profile just as the room lit up a little more with reflected light from the screen.

And she remembered how, back in the day, he had seemed so inaccessible to her somehow. It was why making a play for him had been such a big deal. He'd had charm by the bucketload, looks to turn any female head no matter what age, confidence to burn, a strong family bond behind him no matter what. He'd had everything while she'd had nothing from the moment her nan had got ill.

But knowing he had some tough stuff to work through in the here and now—that he maybe wasn't finding easy to deal with—somehow made him *more human*.

'The lovebirds?' He turned to look down at her, their heads close together as they continued to whisper conspiratorially.

Shannon smiled up at him. 'Yes, that's them. They've been married forty years, barely have a penny—and they're two of the happiest people I've ever met. They look forward to this every week—it's their only night out. Come rain, hail, or sleet they make their way from their little house just up the road to see the film. It's only ever ice or snow that keeps them at home and when that happens someone from here goes to visit them.'

Connor was smiling back at her.

But she couldn't quite manage to keep looking at him when he was doing that, even in the dim, sometimes briefly flashing light. So she looked forwards again.

'When the film's over they have a cup of tea and then they walk home arm in arm. They don't need money to be happy. They value what they have and they make the effort to hang onto it.'

'So now you think I should just give all the money away so I can be happier than I am now?'

The room went dark for a second, so that it took a moment for his face to come into focus when she looked his way. 'I'm not saying that either. It's not up to me to tell you what you should or shouldn't do. Not that you'd let me. I'm just pointing out that being happy isn't necessarily linked to being stupidly rich. Something I think you probably know round about now.'

Connor shook his head.

'And you disagree. That's a nice change.'

He leaned to whisper back, 'Are you still trying to persuade me not to sell this building, perchance?'

If he hadn't said it in such a soft tone then she might have risen to the bait. But, 'Maybe I am. I can't help it, Connor. This place means something.'

'And you're finding it hard to reconcile being attracted to me while technically I'm now the enemy, right?'

'Yes.' Well, it was part of it. So it wasn't a complete lie…

He turned away, his head facing the direction of the older couple again, and Shannon heard him take a deep breath. It was only when his fingers flexed around hers that she remembered she was still holding his hand.

But he didn't answer. And that left Shannon torn for the rest of the film. How could she get involved with him again, even in a purely sexual way, when he was taking something so precious from the people she loved?

CHAPTER SEVEN

'AND THEN THERE were two…'

'Nope, then there was one—I'm gonna have to kick you out. I'm tired and hungry.'

And Shannon needed more time before she slept with him—which was what would happen if he stayed.

Connor shook his head. 'You're not the only one who's hungry. We'll order pizza.'

Shannon mulled that over for a moment or two. Not that she couldn't have done with something to eat, but it would be too dangerous to have him stay. All it would take would be more touching, some kissing, then there would be the removal of clothing, more intimate kissing…

She took a deep breath and blew it out.

'I don't think that's a good idea.'

'You used to like pizza.'

'It has nothing to do with the choice of food.'

Connor's face changed, his dark eyes searching her eyes for a long moment. 'Are you going to try telling me you have a date lined up?'

She could feel yet another flush creep over her cheeks, so she turned away and headed towards the front doors—hoping he would take the hint and follow her. 'No, I don't have a date lined up. I'm just tired. One full day here wasn't enough for you?'

When she turned round he was still standing in the middle of the foyer, his large hands shoved deep into the pockets of his jeans. And he smiled a stunningly sexy smile across at her. 'Maybe I'm just trying to establish where you stand on the whole dating issue.'

'You don't need to know that.'

'Ah, now, you see, that's where you'd be wrong.' Freeing his hands, he walked towards her with slow, measured steps, his gaze still locked on her face. 'I definitely need to know that before I spend another day here.'

The sight of him working his way across the room to her with such a purposeful look on his face sent Shannon's pulse fluttering all over again.

But what she wouldn't and couldn't do was let him see it. It gave him the advantage again. So, she stood her ground—pulling open the door as he got closer.

'Whether or not I have dates lined up has nothing to do with you spending time here to see what this place is all about like you did today. This was a business thing, remember?'

'It may have started out as a business thing. But before we head where we're heading I should at least know whether or not I have to look over my shoulder for rabid boyfriends, don't you think? When we were kissing before the film, that could have been a seven-foot gorilla interrupting us to claim his woman.'

'That wasn't *us* kissing.' She frowned at him as he got closer. 'That was you kissing me to shut me up. I didn't do anything.'

Connor nodded solemnly. 'Only because we were interrupted—we'd have done more than that otherwise. And we're

His eyes gleamed dangerously. 'Oh, I don't know. I think that let's pretend still has a place between consenting adults.'

She reached over to pull the door open. 'And on that note—'

Connor reached out his palm to close the door again, leaning on it so that he was distinctly inside her personal space, his deep voice low and seductive. 'With the building issue to one side, then.'

Shannon found herself mesmerized by the very male lump in his throat, watching it move as he swallowed. 'We can't put it to one side; we're *inside* it as we speak. It's not going away.'

'Well, let's say I made it go away.'

Her gaze shot upwards in surprise. 'Are you saying you'll back out of the sale?'

'No. I told you I wouldn't change my mind that easily. I don't want it. And I still don't get why you won't jump at the chance of a modern building more suited to the things you do here. But maybe, if it's that big a deal to you, you should just *have* the damn thing. And then you won't hide behind it any more.'

Despite the fact that she knew she was doing a really good impersonation of a fish out of water, Shannon continued to stand completely still and stare up at him. He could *not* be serious. People didn't just go around handing entire buildings to other people to settle an argument so the road to sex was clear. Was he *insane?*

'I can't afford to buy this place.'

'I'm a reasonable man, despite what you may think of me.' He smirked. 'I said you could have it. We'll find a nice, long payment plan for you—how does that sound? Because realistically they're like Monopoly houses to me—they don't mean anything beyond one hell of a retirement.'

'How can you *say* something like that? You can't tell me that the business end of that company doesn't mean something to you or you wouldn't be spending so much time working on it. Everything is worth something to somebody. You just don't see places like this as anything beyond their monetary value! And that has to make for a real big empty feeling when you *do* retire, if you don't already feel that way! How can you live your life like that, Connor?'

His expression darkened. 'Well, it's obviously worth something *to you.* Right now, as far as I'm concerned, it's getting in the way, so if handing it to you solves the problem then you can have it. And then we can just stop with the game-playing this time round so we don't make the same mistake we did last time.'

To some people she would have seemed as insane as him for not taking the offer in both hands and running like hell before he changed his mind. But it wasn't that simple, not to Shannon. Or for Connor, no matter what he thought. And that was before she even *thought* about visiting the subject of the game *he thought* she had played last time!

'Is your life really that unsatisfying now that you have to bargain a building to me for sex?'

'What kind of question is that?'

She folded her arms again. 'I don't think this whole—' then unfolded them to make invisible speech marks in the air '—"destroy Frank's legacy" mission you claim to be on is your real problem, is it?'

'I already told you I don't want any part of what mattered to him.'

'You might not want it, Connor, but you've got it. And believe it or not—in this world—with the company he left you comes responsibility. Or at least that's the way it should be. Responsibility to your own soul's well-being if not to the people whose lives and livelihoods rely heavily on the decisions you make every day! And you should know that coming from the background you came from—where it was people and family and caring that made the real difference—so this new attitude of yours doesn't make any sense, which means that the money and the company and the buildings aren't the real problem. The problem is inside you!'

Pushing back off the door, he nodded once towards her feet. 'Do you want a soapbox to stand on to continue this or should I just pull up a chair?'

O-h-h, that was *it!* Using all of her body weight, she reached her hands out to his broad chest and shoved—hard. And it was so unexpected a move that she did actually manage to rock him back a step before he grabbed hold of her hands and pushed upright again—in time for her to stand on tiptoe to get 'in his face' properly.

'No matter what mistakes Frank McMahon made in his life, he at least made something of it! And whether or not you care about that doesn't matter—because the man is *dead!* The only person you're letting down by being such a moron is yourself!'

Connor swore. 'And I'm getting yelled at for giving you the one thing you've argued with me most over ever since I've got here! How does *that* make any sense?'

'Maybe—*unlike you*—I get more satisfaction out of building something good and decent and worthwhile. Something that makes a difference to people's lives! Because when I wake up each day I have to look at myself in the mirror. Can you do that, Connor? Can you look yourself in the mirror and like what you see there? What happened to the man who built a business from the ground with his brother—the one who helped support an entire family when they needed it—the one who must have worked night and day to make sure it worked? Who cared that much! Where is *he?*'

'And your life is so perfect, is it? Hiding away here in this wreck of a place with a load of pensioners, a gay best friend, and other people's kids? I wouldn't go throwing any stones if I were you!'

Shannon's heart cracked open a little inside of her. 'When a single bit of my life is any concern of yours then you can go right on ahead and make judgements!'

'That goes both ways, don't you think?'

'Well, now that we both know exactly where we stand, why don't you just leave, Connor? Go away. Go make someone else's life difficult—I'm sure there are thousands of people living in Devenish buildings who'll be ecstatic to see you coming!'

But he leaned in closer, his expression dangerously dark, hands holding hers in a viselike grip as he told her in a strained voice, 'You know your problem, Shannon? It bugs you that you want me as much as you do, that's what this is really about. If that kiss hadn't been interrupted earlier we could have been upstairs using all this energy a *much* better way. You know that whatever was between us before is still here—in all its varying forms of complication. And it *kills* you that that might mean stepping outside of this safe little world you've made for yourself!'

The loud sound of their ragged breathing filled the short pause before he swore again, throwing her hands back from his chest, opening his mouth to say more—and then completely stunning Shannon by yanking open the door and stalking out through it.

Leaving her alone in the sudden silence.

After a moment she sagged back against the wall, staring into space, trying to figure out what had just happened.

She had just said things to him that had to have been very hurtful to him if his life really did feel at all empty. Of all people, *she* should know that—because he'd been right about her fear of stepping outside the safe little world she'd found. Not that she could ever begin to explain to him why. And yet she had thrown the words in his face to hit back at him regardless—leaving him little choice but to throw equally angry words back at her.

Every cruel, hurtful truth he had said in return had only been what she deserved. She'd made this mess, had probably laid the foundations for it seven years ago.

Why? Why couldn't she just leave him be to make his own mistakes? To learn on his own? How could it still matter to her so much?

It *was* the physical attraction addling her brain, wasn't it? It had to be. It couldn't be anything else.

If she had to find one thing she could blame her erratic mood swings on, then surely that would be it? Because from that first dance, hell, from the first day he had walked in looking so disgustingly sexy in his expensive suit, she had had to deal with her reaction on the most basic of physical levels. And having spent all evening with her body pressed alongside his, well—

But now she was left feeling so overwhelmingly alone and empty—and frustrated. It was almost as if, in the space of one full day in his company, he had become a part of her life again in all the ways that had made her want him so badly before.

Would she ever be able to just reach out and grab hold of something when she wanted it without worrying about the repercussions? Maybe if the repercussion hadn't been so life changing the last time…

But surely the one time would have done it? Sex for sex's sake, for mutual satisfaction and the removal of tension, maybe even to eradicate some of the haunting memories from before—at least for Shannon.

But any chance of that had just walked out the door, along with any chance of saving her building.

All those people that relied on her—all those people that she would now have to sit down to explain how she had lost them the one lifeline they had in their cash-strapped community—they'd be devastated.

Lifting her hands, she pressed the fleshy part of her palms tight in against her eyes, leaning over while she tried to even out her breathing. On top of everything else she really couldn't allow herself to have a panic attack, or—worse still—to cry…

After a few breaths she pushed up and off the wall, yanking open the inner door to step into the small vestibule so that she could lock the outer door. She reached into the pocket of her sweats to find the key, looked up—and gasped when she found Connor looking back at her through the glass.

The last of a glorious summer's day was dying in the sky behind him while he stared at her, his jaw line clenching while he thought. And on the other side of the door Shannon stood transfixed, holding her breath, waiting to see what he was going to do next.

'Open the door.'

Shannon shook her head and he scowled in response.

'Open the door, Shannon.'

She shook her head again. 'It's not locked.'

Stating the obvious tore a small smile from him, before he glanced away, looked heavenwards, and then pulled open the door, stepping into the small space she made for him when she stepped back.

Towering over her again, he searched her wide eyes for a long moment, watching as she pursed her lips together to stop saying something that might start another argument.

Then he took a breath. 'I wasn't trying to give you what you wanted to make things worse.'

'I kn—'

He held up a hand. 'No—don't say a word. Let's not do any more damage, okay?'

Shannon pursed her lips again.

While the hand in front of her curled until he had a forefinger to point at her. '*You*—are capable of making me angrier—' his hand uncurled again as he held both hands out in a sweeping movement '—than *any other* woman on this planet. I have *no idea* why that is you can do that.'

She pursed her lips even tighter together. Because that statement was just *begging* for an answer.

'But what beats me even more is that I keep coming back, every time.' He took a deep, steadying breath, glancing briefly upwards again. 'All right, so I'm not perfect, but you've known me a long time, so you've always known that. And, frankly, I have no interest in being perfect 'cos that's a lot of pressure to put on yourself. So, yeah, occasionally I *am* going to mess up—like I *apparently* did five minutes ago when I tried to remove this great pink elephant that always seems to be standing between us communicating.'

Shannon swallowed hard and allowed her mouth to relax. Because she genuinely didn't want another argument with him, and when he was making this big a gesture by staying to talk it through with her there was just no way she was going to do anything to spoil it. She even tried a small smile of encouragement on for size.

Which brought his gaze to her mouth for a long, long while before he swallowed hard, locked eyes with her again, and his voice became huskier. 'The thing about being a crusader, Shannon, is that you have to have a "She who casts the first stone" quality to you. I could say plenty about you building some kind of stand-in family for yourself here rather than making one of your own with someone—'

Oh, and that *had* to be answered!

But he raised a hand again as her mouth opened. 'No, now you *know* that's true. Don't bother denying it. Many things I may be, but blind isn't one of them.'

She resorted to scowling up at him instead.

'It's like this. Neither of us are necessarily doing a good job with our lives right now this second. But you can't make me find my path—that I'll do on my own—which, right now, leaves me with just the *one* problem to deal with…'

Her eyebrows rose in question.

And finally he smiled a small smile in return. 'Aren't you going to ask me what that problem might be?'

'Oh, I'm allowed to speak now am I?'

'Yes, you are.'

'That's gracious of you.' She smiled to negate the sarcasm in her words. 'So, what *is* your problem?'

'You. *You're* my problem.'

The answer took her breath away, said with such intensity

in his voice and his eyes that she was left in no doubt that his inner struggle was as torturous as her own.

Placing them on equal ground for the first time.

'You see—' he took a step closer '—while I seem to have this inability to stay away from you for long and together we seem to have this ability for ending up in an argument of some kind or another every damn time—I'm left with a real problem deciding whether to strangle you or kiss you senseless. Because you have to know as well as I do that most of this arguing comes down to one thing.'

'And that is?' She knew the answer before he said it.

'It's sexual tension. What we ended on last time is exactly what we've started with this time. We're not done. We're nowhere near done.'

Shannon damped her lips with the end of her tongue, watching him watch the movement with heavy eyes and without taking the time to think about the repercussions—she dived right in with the one choice that her pulse rate would be happy with. Her chin rose in challenge.

'Well, I don't want to be strangled.'

Connor's hands reached up to frame her face, his long fingers threading deep into the thick hair at her nape while his head lowered until his warm breath was fanning her lips. 'Good choice.'

CHAPTER EIGHT

THIS TIME THERE was no question about Shannon not joining in. No question at all—regardless of where it would take her. She'd deal with the damn consequences later.

The door key she had been holding made a loud jangle as it hit the tiled floor. But Shannon couldn't hear anything beyond the roaring in her ears, couldn't feel anything but the pressure of Connor's mouth on hers. She barely even noticed the taste of Dolly Mixtures in his mouth.

He was right. They weren't done. Nowhere near it.

That one unmatched night of sheer passion had never left her memory. But the experience had been overshadowed by so much sadness afterwards that she now wanted nothing more than to overshadow the shadows with more of that same passion. She'd just been kidding herself she didn't want that from the very second he'd walked in the door, hadn't she?

It *was* why she couldn't leave things be, why she argued with him so much. She'd been fighting against something she had no control over—she'd never had control of it.

Her hands bunched into tight fistfuls of shirt against his chest while she moved her head to keep her mouth constantly on his. And she felt dizzy for a second as the memory of his kisses invaded her mind, tangling the past and present together so that it was tough to know what was then and what was now.

The moment he ran his tongue over her bottom lip she sighed, opening up to him. Kissing him was *good!*

But it wasn't enough. Not when her body already knew what could follow.

Instinctively her hands flattened, smoothing over the broad expanse of muscled chest, then lower—where she felt his stomach muscles contract. And when he dragged his mouth briefly from hers, she smiled as he grumbled down at her. 'Slowly.'

Standing up on tiptoe, she continued smiling against his mouth. 'We did slowly last time.'

'And slowly worked if I recall.' He pushed her back against the cool plaster wall, his head descending to the sensitive skin below her ear where his tongue flickered out to taste her and tease her even more.

Shannon raised her arms, frantically tangling her fingers in his short hair to draw his head up to see his face. When his eyebrows rose in question she told him firmly, 'When we last did this I was a twenty-year-old virgin—slow was exactly what I needed. I'm a fully grown twenty-seven-year-old woman now who has just had a massive row with you. What we're about to do is make-up sex. Make-up sex isn't slow.'

Connor grinned wickedly. 'And I thought we were just kissing…'

'We've never *just* kissed.'

At some point, while they'd been 'just kissing', he had let go of her face, his hands dropping to her hips to hold her in place. And while she had her arms raised he took advantage of the unrestricted access to her body, smoothing up her sides until his thumbs were underneath her breasts.

'Make-up sex, huh?' He looked down at his thumbs as they rose, tracing the lace of her bra through the thin material of her T-shirt. 'You might have to show me how that goes, because I've never actually stayed in a relationship long enough for that.'

Shannon was looking at him in disbelief when he glanced up, a wicked gleam in his eyes. 'But then, like I said, I've never actually argued with someone the way I end up arguing with you.'

His mouth stole the gasp from her lips when he cupped her breasts, kneading through the soft material, gently at first, then with more pressure, until Shannon thought her knees would buckle underneath her. She moaned in protest when he stopped, twisting her head back and forth when he began to tug the T-shirt upwards, freeing it from the waistband of her sweats.

Eventually he tore his mouth free to grumble, 'Where did you drop the key?'

'What key?' There was a key?

'The key to the door—we really need to move away from here. 'Cos I'm fairly sure that we can be seen from the street.'

Shannon swore softly. You'd have thought that, as the one who lived there, that thought might have occurred to her. If they stayed where they were for much longer, doing what they were doing, then any passer-by was in for one hell of a show.

But it gave her a moment to pause for thought—to seek some sense of rationale. She could stop this if she wanted to.

To hell with that!

When he kissed her again, this time harder and with more unbridled raw passion than before, she knew she was already lost.

She wrenched her mouth free when she couldn't get enough air into her lungs. 'I dropped it. It must be on the floor.'

They pulled apart long enough to find the key, lock the door, and push back through the inner door to the foyer. And by then they were already wrapped around each other again, lips tangled while they fumbled frantically to remove layers of clothing.

'Are you sure everyone has gone home? No Yummy Mummies or Briedas to appear from behind one of those doors?'

Shannon's answer was as breathless as Connor's question had been while she kicked off her shoes and hauled his shirt down over his elbows. 'Positive.'

She disappeared briefly underneath her T-shirt as Connor pulled it over her head. Then he took a long moment to kiss her senseless again while he deftly unhooked her bra and slid the scrap of material off her shoulders.

It was only then, as he stood back a little from her and watched his hands on her naked breasts, that everything slowed down a little.

And in the silence of the room their ragged breathing and the thundering of his heart in his chest made Connor feel as if it was a moment he would never forget.

Just as the last time had been.

He splayed his fingers, studying the contrast between his tanned skin and her pale breasts. When he held his fingers wide that way he could hold each breast completely within his palm—which was sexy as hell—and the sense of urgency came back in a single heartbeat.

He needed desperately to be inside her. He'd waited long enough.

She moved her hands up his arms, grasping hold of his

shoulders to rock back a little on her heels, pushing her breasts tighter into his hands. And the sight of her arched towards him like that was as much as he could take, his erection straining agonizingly against the buttons of his jeans.

He sought her lips again, plunging his tongue into the sweet-tasting recesses of her mouth in a way that could leave her in no doubt of what he wanted. And she met him kiss for kiss, touch for touch, her hands frantic on his back, grasping hold of his shoulders, nails digging into his skin as she moaned into his mouth.

'We're never going to make it up four flights of stairs.' He looked around the foyer.

Reluctantly he freed her breasts, wrapping his arms around her narrow waist to lift her off the ground and march them behind the large counter, while Shannon's hair brushed against his chin as she looked to see where he was taking her.

Using his forearm to clear a space on the lower shelf, he hoisted her higher, groaning at the delicious sensation of her soft breasts crushing against his hard chest, before he unceremoniously plunked her down, smiling at her as she grinned up at him.

'Right here?'

'We've gone past the window of opportunity for slow. And I told you that kitchen counter has been on my mind for days now. So, yes, *right here.*'

Leaning down, he kissed her again, plunging his tongue deep into her mouth while one hand reached for her breast again, the other snaking lower, turning over, so that his knuckles grazed over her flat stomach and along the edge of her white lace panties.

Drawing another low moan from her throat to echo around the cavernous room. But when she reached out for the button on the band of his jeans he stepped back out of her reach, wrenching his mouth free to rest his forehead against hers for a moment.

'You do that and you really are going to end up with the hard and fast version of this.'

Almost panting, she looked up into his eyes. 'I want hard and fast. We just had a fight, remember?'

'I remember. But we both need to be at the same place. I want you to come when I'm inside you.'

He watched in amazement as she smiled a purely sexual smile up at him, her eyes gazing into his up close and personal as she whispered, 'Who says I'm not at the same place you are? I want you inside me. *Now.*'

Connor didn't need much more of an invitation, but he needed to be sure she was ready for him, so he slipped an investigative finger beneath the lace—and found liquid, molten heat. With his eyes still focused on hers, he watched her eyelids grow heavy, saw her arching her head back from him as she moaned again.

He'd known it would be like this with them, hadn't he? Had known it from the moment he had seen her on the dance floor of that small bar his first night in Galway. The first time had been unforgettable, but this was unforgettable on a whole new level. Who wouldn't want a woman like this?

'I remember this.'

He stepped in closer again, his finger sliding back and forth inside her as she arched into his touch. 'I remember what it felt like to have you naked against me.'

Shannon's head dropped back further, her body bowing up from the counter as she made small sighs and gasps of pleasure.

'I remember those noises you're making right now.'

Using his knuckles to stretch the lace a little more, he ran his fingertip up and circled her—the touch eliciting an upward buck of her hips towards him.

She rocked forwards, her forehead against his chest as she gasped out, 'Please tell me you have a condom with you.'

'In my wallet—back pocket. Lift your hips for me.'

It seemed to take for ever for her to find the condom in his wallet, while he took an equal amount of for ever slowly removing the last scrap of lace from her body. And all the while Shannon had her head tilted back enough for her glorious curls of long blonde hair to cascade over her shoulders while she smiled up at him.

And Connor suddenly realized that that wasn't an echo of an image from his memory. This one was new. Last time she had had that sultry outfit on so that he hadn't been looking at Shannon, not really, just glimpses of her. This time he could see the corkscrew curl he was so fond of plastered against her damp cheek, he could see the smile on her swollen lips, the slow blinking of her stunning green eyes. He wasn't looking at a fantasy version of Shannon. This time she was trusting herself to him completely.

And he felt ridiculously humbled by that.

Smiling down at her, he reached forward to take the foil packet from her fingers. But Shannon shook her head, her hair moving in waves as she damped her lips again.

'I'll do it.'

'That's not a good idea. I'm hanging by a thread here as it is.'

She shook her head again.

Shedding his jeans and boxers he grasped hold of the counter on either side of her, his arms flexing as he gritted his teeth to fight for control while she rolled the condom onto him, her eyes focused completely on the task. 'It's always going to be a battle of wills with us, even over the little things, isn't it?'

She tilted her head forwards, her lips against the taut column of his neck as her small hand encircled his raging erection. 'Nothing little about it.'

Sidling forwards on the counter, her heels brushing up the back of his calves, she shook her hair back and looked up at him, her eyes studying his for the longest time. And she held the simple unspoken contact with him as he lifted his arms, placing one hand in the small of her back and one in her hair, as he slowly slid into her slick warmth.

Shannon drew in a long, slow gasp of air as she took in every inch of him, until he was buried as deep as he could go.

And Connor closed his eyes for a moment, lost in the sensation of her body sheathing his. There was no barrier this time; her gasp wasn't an indication of the brief pain she had experienced losing her virginity before. When he opened his eyes she was staring up at him, her hands whispering against his skin.

For that brief moment Connor's heart stopped. She was truly, truly amazing. It was true that no other woman had ever made him angrier. But it was also true that no other woman had ever had him so hot so fast.

She was *amazing.*

'I remember this too.' He flexed his hips, drawing back until he had almost left her, then sliding back until his pelvis hit hers, tilting his head to look down as he repeated the movement, watching the way her stomach was sucked inwards every time he slid home.

Lifting a hand from his side, she cupped the side of his face, biting down on her bottom lip as he slid back and forwards again, damping her lips before she angled his face up and drew him down for another searing kiss. 'I remember too—all of it—this most of all.'

Already he could feel her beginning to clamp around him, her inner muscles tightening as she got closer to release. It was the sweetest kind of torture, the answering build of tension in his abdomen, the most basic of male responses. But with Shannon tearing her mouth from his to rest her forehead against his chin, breathing in sharp gasps, Connor felt something else build inside him. Something he didn't recognize; something almost painful.

But they were too far gone for him to take time out to think about it or to try and pin a name to it while he increased the pace, heard her moans growing louder as her damp body arched back from him. So close. He was so close.

'Shannon—'

'I know.' She silenced him with another kiss. '*I know.* Don't stop.'

She kissed him again. And again. And when he reached a hand between their slick bodies to touch a fingertip to her sensitive nub, she cried out against his mouth, her body convulsing inside and out as her release pulled him over the edge.

And she kissed him again. And on and on until they both had to stop for breath, foreheads touching, eyes fixed on each other's. Then, as the rippling sensations ebbed, Connor smiled again, slower this time, wrapping his arms around her slender frame to draw her closer against him.

'Oh, yeah, definitely a fan of make-up sex.'

Shannon laughed, her sweet breath washing cool air over his heated skin. 'That's just as well considering the way we argue.'

'We could have been doing this for the last seven years, you know.'

'No, we couldn't.' Her hands smoothed up his back while she tilted her head back to look up at him, wearing a more serious expression on her face. 'But you were right; we weren't done with this.'

Connor frowned at her reasoning, more irritated by her swift dismissal of a potential relationship than he could ever remember being with any woman before. In fact, he'd dated women before who, if they'd even mentioned the 'R' word, would have had him on the run pretty damn fast. But this was Shannon, and even if he hadn't found his way in other portions of his life or even decided what in hell he was going to do with it in the long term—he knew he wanted her in it in the here and now.

In the meantime he picked on the one thing she had said that he agreed with. 'No, and we're still not done.'

When he kissed her this time it was slow and deliberate, placing a seal on his words, because he had meant them. Figuring out how to make everything work could come somewhere along the line, he reckoned.

'Do you have to go or are you staying?'

He smiled softly at the question. 'I have to go meet some of the guys from the gym at six to go hang-gliding.'

Shannon rolled her eyes. 'Course you do.'

'No, really, I do. We have a gym here in the city and when I visited the other day we arranged to do a team-building trip. It's not an excuse to not stay the night.'

She frowned in confusion. 'You have a gym in Galway?'

'Yep. And technically I still own half the business so I dropped in to see how they were doing.'

'How long has it been open?'

'Nearly a year.'

'Did you set it up or do you hire people to do that?'

His fingers absentmindedly played with his favourite curl while he answered. 'I do all the set-ups for the new places. When Rory was overseas I did General Manager between the three we had but since he came home we've split it between us and expanded.'

She was still frowning.

'What?'

'You were here when I arrived in Galway.'

'Was I?'

She nodded, then leaned forwards and kissed him again. 'Small world. And now I'm starting to get cold.'

'Maybe we should try and find all our clothes before anyone else does?'

The idea made her laugh. And Connor laughed with her—he could just imagine how that would go down with the Briedas of her world!

'It would certainly be less embarrassing than coming down here in the morning to explain, yes.'

After another loud smacking kiss, Connor pulled away from her, bending to lift his jeans and pull on his boxers. Then together they searched around to find all the items they had discarded along the way, rewarding each rediscovered item with another kiss.

Another thought occurred to him. 'What are you doing on Monday night?'

'We're quiet on Monday. Why?' Her eyes sparkled with mischief from across the room as she hauled her T-shirt over her head, her voice muffled for a second. 'Do you have something for us to argue about so we can make up?'

He didn't answer for a second while he watched her breasts lift upwards as she raised her arms. Though she'd obviously lost weight at some point, judging by the almost invisible fine lines he could see on her stomach, all the varying sports and activities she had studied in America had left her more toned than she'd been before she'd left. But she still had more than enough curves to fill his eye and he looked upwards for a second to thank whoever was responsible for that.

He assumed a straight face before she reappeared from behind her mussed hair. 'If we get to make up after then I'll think of something we can *debate.* But I have a do to go to—so come with me.'

'What sort of a do?'

He shrugged. 'Just a do. I'd tell you more but it would take away the mystery of it. When two people have known each other as long as we have it's important to keep working on that, I feel.' He discovered his last shoe and pushed it on before stepping across and kissing her one last time, smiling down at her when he lifted his head. 'So I'll see you Monday. It'll be a date. We never tried one of those before.'

Shannon stared at him for a long while, the 'something' that had been so elusive earlier in the day briefly making a reappearance before she answered him, 'All right. What should I wear?'

'My preference will always be nothing. So I'm not the right person to ask that question.'

CHAPTER NINE

THE PARCEL ARRIVED Monday morning, causing quite a stir. Mainly because Shannon hadn't been there to sign for it and it had become the focus of much debate in her absence—so that by the time she returned it had a small guard of honour.

'Delivery for you, sugar lump!' Mario beckoned her over with a rapidly gesturing hand. 'And you have to open it here so we can all see what it is. The curiosity has been killing us!'

Shannon scowled at the flat box when there was enough of a gap for her to see it. 'I didn't order anything.'

'Honey, if this came from the shop named on the delivery docket you couldn't *afford* to order anything.'

His flare for the dramatic was almost legendary, so Shannon ignored the glee on her friend's face and studied the box. She was almost afraid to touch it. Especially if it had come from where she thought it had come from.

Not that he had bothered his backside picking up a phone in two days.

Which had left her feeling more than a tad annoyed—well, furious would be more accurate. She'd been in a foul mood for most of the weekend because of it, and it hadn't gone unnoticed either. So much for dealing with the consequences of her actions!

'C'mon and open it. It might cheer you up!'

Yep. And it was Mario who had been *pointing out* her mood all weekend. He'd tried to pry the gory details out of her. But she wasn't ready to talk about Connor to *anyone*. Where would she begin?

'Well, actually we had a row after the film and then great make-up sex.'

Not that 'great' was the right description. Yes, the sex itself had been great there was no arguing that—it had been better than great. What had caused her almost obsessive angst ever since had been what *hadn't* been so great about it. For starters she had the old sex-versus-making-love debate going on in her head…

Two people who cared about each other didn't just have sex. That was what it said in all the women's magazines, right? And there was no doubt in Shannon's mind that what they had had was great, hot, mutually satisfying sex. The tension that had been building between them from argument to argument had been based in the sexual relationship they had that obviously wasn't over and done with yet. Just as Connor had said. It had been there ever since he'd come back—bubbling under the surface—simmering away until it had to have a natural release of some kind or another, right?

But it wasn't the same as the first time. When they *had* made love. And it hadn't taken away the magical quality of that night, or any of the agony that had followed it.

If anything, it had made things worse.

Her eyes still on the box, she began to tug off her coat, walking around the counter to put it away while Mario practically danced from foot to foot with excitement.

'If you don't open that thing in the next two seconds I swear *I* will!'

'He's been like a child at Christmas since it arrived.'

Shannon glanced up at the sound of a familiar voice, smiling a genuine smile when she saw the young woman's face. 'Hello, Mary. It's good to see you again. How's the baby? Did you bring her with you?'

'Yes, she's asleep in her pushchair—'

'And you can see her *after* you open the box…' Mario tapped it with his index finger. '*Box*—remember?'

All eyes refocused on it while Shannon sent a silent prayer upwards that there was nothing too personal in it. Especially if it *was* from Connor, double especially after the make-up sex. Who knew what he might have put in there?

With a flex of her fingers, she leaned forwards and undid the straps, lifting the lid to discover layers of tissue underneath—with an envelope on top.

Shannon stared at it as if touching it might burn her.

'Oh, for goodness' sake!' It was unceremoniously pushed into her hand. 'Just read it!'

She stepped back while she opened it. To find a familiar scrawl on a piece of white card.

'For tonight Sunshine. Will be there 7.30.'

'It's from *him,* isn't it?'

'From who?' Mary grinned at Mario's beaming face. 'Has Shannon met a man? I knew I'd miss something good while I was in hospital—it's always the way.'

With a deep breath, and her heart beating erratically in her chest, she stepped forwards again to push back the layer of tissue paper.

'Oh, what a gorgeous dress!' Mary and her friend oohed

and ahhed before Shannon even had it out of the box, 'It looks really expensive.'

'When you have a millionaire for a boyfriend, then money's not a problem.' Mario peered down at the label. 'Oh, dear, another Dior. You have a wardrobe stuffed with those already. *Not.*'

As he lifted it with a flourish from the box Shannon continued to stare in silence. It was the most beautiful thing she had ever seen, even held up in front of a six-foot lunatic wearing a Gay Pride T-shirt.

A deep emerald green, the material shimmered in the light, so soft that even the minuscule airflow in the foyer made it shift back and forth like a whisper. And it would feel like that against her skin too, wouldn't it? Wearing that dress for the evening would be foreplay again when she was in Connor's company.

'He must be taking you somewhere nice.'

She finally managed to mumble back an answer. 'I have no idea. All he said was it was a "do".'

'If this dress is anything to go by, then I bet I know what "do" he was referring to.'

Her gaze shifted to the smug expression above the dress. 'What is it?'

'Hottest ticket in town if you move in the right circles.' The glare she gave him was apparently enough for him to continue. 'It's the launch of the new wing at the museum—part of the celebration for Galway's bid for European City of Culture. Your gorgeous man won't be the only millionaire there, I bet. And with you in this dress he'll have a job keeping them away from you.'

Shannon shook her head, reaching out to touch the material of the dress. It was beautiful. The most beautiful thing anyone had ever given her. And it was from *Connor.*

He had looked at this dress and thought of her in it. And that thought made her smile.

Dolly Mixtures and Dior. It was a potent combination.

'I don't know that I can do this dress justice.' She reluctantly folded it back into the box, stroking her palm over it lovingly. *Connor* had bought her a *Dior dress.* It was surreal. 'I've never worn something this beautiful.'

Somewhere in her furtive imagination, it briefly felt like payment for Friday night. But that was ridiculous, and she knew it was a callous thing for her to think, even for a second.

She just felt so empty inside.

She could pinpoint the beginning of her awareness of that emptiness to when he had told her he had been in Galway when she'd arrived there. He had probably been there for months while she'd looked for a place to live, while she'd tentatively begun to open her heart to a brand-new group of friends, while she'd tried for once to allow herself to fill the void she'd had inside ever since America.

He'd been here in Galway, living his life without her—had maybe even passed her in the street or on a sunny day in Eyre Square and not even noticed she was there.

When she'd purposefully picked Galway to make sure she would never have to bump into him again.

Knowing he had been there had made her ache and that was when she had first felt the emptiness. Even when he had been inside her, filling her body and sending her spiralling off the edge, there had still been something missing—something that might have helped fill that emptiness.

Mario's hands were on her shoulders, shaking her, 'That is the daftest thing I've ever heard you say! When I'm done with your makeover everyone will think you do the gardening in Dior—you just wait and see.'

Shannon smiled a small smile. '*No one* gardens in Dior. I'm sure you can be shot for that kind of sacrilege.'

'Someone somewhere probably does.' He shook her again. 'You just listen, my girl. Cinders will go to the ball with Prince Charming whether she likes it or not. And when Cinders has the prince wrapped around her little finger she can just persuade him to hand back the nice derelict wreck we all love and adore. And then all the hair-straightening, eyebrow plucking, leg waxing agony I'm about to put you through will all seem worthwhile.'

The smile became a grimace, but not for the reasons Mario probably assumed. Because Prince Charming had already tried to hand back the building, hadn't he? And Cinders had basically told him to *stick it!*

It didn't really matter if she got to the end of the evening feeling even emptier than she already did. If nothing else came out of what was going on between her and Connor, she had to somehow try and make sure the people she loved weren't caught in the fallout. Even if accepting the building meant she might feel that, somehow, she had paid for it with sex.

One night in a Dior given to her by the man she had once loved couldn't make things any worse than they already were, right?

C'mon! After all—it was Dior. What was a girl *supposed* to do?

Shannon's transformation became a group effort as the day progressed. So that by the time she was standing outside the front door looking down at Connor, she did feel a bit like Cinderella.

And if she was, then Connor sure filled the other role to

perfection. He was *sensational* in a tux! Even with his short hair spiking and a bad-boy gleam in his eyes. Rock star chic—that was what it was. And he wore it *so* well! He could have been born in one of those things…

Lifting one side of her long skirt, she tilted her chin down to make sure she didn't fall on her way down the steps. It felt like years since she'd last worn heels so ridiculous and impractical to walk in. And shoes were normally her one foray into the ridiculous and the impractical. When she could afford them.

As she finally stood in front of him he grinned broadly at her. 'Nice dress.'

Shannon lifted her nose and blinked disdainfully at him to cover any sense of discomfort she felt as he looked her down and then back up—with torturous deliberation. 'It's Dior as it happens.'

'Is it now?' He nodded at her, his grin still in place. 'Just something you had hanging around from all those other millionaires you know in Galway?'

She smiled at the memory from their first conversation. How had he remembered that?

'My other designer dresses are in the dry-cleaner's.' She stared at him for a moment and then turned on her heel to give him the full effect of his purchase. 'Will I do?'

'You'll more than do. You look *stunning*.' His dark eyes swept upwards, the grin fading as he examined her hair. 'What have you done to your hair?'

One hand automatically rose to the back of her head to make sure it hadn't fallen out of the chignon 'masterpiece'. 'Mario spent two hours straightening it and putting it up, so I'm under strict instructions to tell you that if so much as one drop of rain touches my head I will "poof up" into the frizz I normally live with.'

'Well, then, let's give him a fright shall we?' He stepped in closer. 'Cos he's watching, isn't he?'

Her green eyes widened. 'Oh, you *cannot* touch the hair.'

'Well, that's a given, but it doesn't mean I can't kiss you and make him think I *might* touch the hair.'

When he leaned closer she leaned back, avoiding his mouth. But it had nothing to do with not wanting to frighten her hairstylist. 'You'll ruin my make-up.'

Connor's eyes narrowed at her excuse. Then he nodded, just the once, before stepping back to open the car door for her. 'Just so you know, that "Get Out Of Jail" card is only valid for use once—at the *start* of the night.'

There was silence for a while as Connor pulled the car out, focusing all his attention on getting them off the cobbled street and onto a wider road. But once they were moving properly he glanced across at her.

And she managed only half a smile.

Which made him frown briefly. 'Is something wrong?'

'No. Why would there be anything wrong?'

'Now, you see, I know you well enough to know that's a lie. So what did I manage to do to make you mad when I wasn't even here?'

She glanced across at his profile as he made a turn. 'Maybe I'm just nervous about going to the "do" of the year. It's not like I make a habit of wearing designer dresses and mixing with the rich and famous.'

Connor's mouth twitched as he glanced at her from the corner of his eye. 'How do you know that's where I'm taking you? It's supposed to be a surprise.'

'Are you telling me that's *not* where we're going?'

The twitch became a smile. 'I don't believe you're nervous. Nothing fazes you.'

'Well, then, maybe you don't know me as well as you think you do. Lots of things faze me, *every day.* It's a fact of life for most people.'

'Like what, for instance?'

'You need a *list?*'

'An example would do.'

The temptation to cross her arms was agonizing. But there was no way she was going to crease her dress. She even missed the stupid curl she was always pushing away—at least it gave her something to do with her hands.

'One little one. Go on, give it a go. It's called sharing. People do that when they get involved, I'm told.'

Involved? She blinked at him. But when it was met with another smile she gave up and stared out of the dark-tinted windscreen, searching her mind for a non-Connor-related-faze-her topic to share as an example. 'Large families faze me.'

So much for the non-Connor part. It was getting to the stage where nigh on everything kept coming back to him, didn't it?

'That's not true. I come from a large family and they never fazed you—it was like you'd always been there from the first day Tess brought you home from school.'

It was a tad close to the bone to discuss anything related to their past. From the time when everything in her life had been so wrapped up in him. As it was getting to be in the here and now.

'No, they fazed me. For years.' She took a deep breath and let it out. 'To someone like me, a family like yours—the way you all are together—well... Let's put it like this—it's like going into a room where everyone is laughing at a joke and

I'm the only one that doesn't get what's funny. Only all of you all knew the joke from birth so when you try to explain it to me, you only say the punchline, expecting I'll get it—so there's no way I'll *ever* understand. Even after years of going in and out of your house I still didn't completely get it, no matter how much I wanted to or how many times I tried asking someone to explain it to me. Eventually I understood *most* of it. But I never laughed the way you guys all did. And I felt left out. *That* fazed me.'

Connor went silent for a long while as Shannon hid the expanding emptiness inside her with another smile. 'You see, I knew you wouldn't get that. Why would you? You knew the joke.'

'It's not that I don't understand. It's just you put it into a very clever, if rambling, analogy and it's going to take me a minute to think up one as smart.' He glanced her way again as he made another turn, smiling at her in a way that almost looked affectionate. 'You do know that you babble when you're nervous too, right?'

Shannon frowned. He knew her better than she liked to think he did.

His deep voice dropped an octave as he reached across to wrap his fingers around her cold hand. 'What you're saying is that you always felt like an outsider? Right?'

'Probably. A little.'

'Well, let me just put something straight, Sunshine—you were never an outsider. Everyone loved you.'

Everyone except the one person she had wanted to love her. But she couldn't say that, could she? And as they pulled up outside the museum the emptiness inside her almost doubled her over.

Connor parked the car, turning in his seat to look at her with a thoughtful expression—until she could take no more. 'What now?'

'Look at me.'

Forcing strength into her spine, she turned to face him, her eyelashes slowly rising until her gaze locked with his. And the air tingled between them as it always did, his sensual mouth curving up into a smile that sent hundreds of lights flickering through the dark depths of his eyes. It wasn't fair. Men like him weren't supposed to exist outside female sexual fantasies—they really weren't. It wasn't that he was perfect, she knew that. But he was Connor. And there was just something about him that had always fascinated her—drawn her in—made her want *more.*

So much more than he had ever been able to give her.

She watched in silence as a large hand rose to her face as it had so often of late, his fingertips stroking tenderly against her cheek, his hand turning—knuckles grazing along her jaw and down the column of her neck.

And when he spoke his voice was husky. 'You look very beautiful tonight. And there isn't a single person that won't turn to look when you walk through those doors—'

'Not helping with the nervous thing.'

Connor chuckled. 'You meet people every day, Shannon. You talk to them, listen to them. It's what you do—so just be yourself.' He leaned closer. 'And trust me—if I hadn't already said I would be here, then we would be heading to my hotel right now and we wouldn't be leaving the room for the next twenty-four hours.'

Truth was, any nervousness she had probably had less to do with where they were or who they might meet than it had to do with the prospect of another night in his arms. Having sex—not making love.

But it wasn't as if she could tell him *that.*

He leaned further across the centre console, a wicked smile in place. 'Sooner we go inside, the sooner we can leave.'

Shannon's eyes narrowed, despite the smile she could feel growing on her face. It was just so difficult to focus when he was like this—so charming and persuasive and damned tempting and with that silent amusement in his eyes.

Yeah, he had her and he knew it, didn't he?

She should hate his guts for that ability to draw her in every single time. But she didn't hate him.

And as he leaned in to mess up her make-up a little Shannon had a sudden realization.

Not hating him any more was the biggest problem of all, wasn't it?

CHAPTER TEN

CONNOR COULDN'T TAKE his eyes off Shannon. And he couldn't remember ever being so proud of the way that one person could manage to look so confident, so beautiful and yet so unaware of how beautiful she was. She was truly amazing.

Her small hand had been cold inside his warm grasp when they had first walked in, and she had clung to him through the first introductions and conversations. Selfishly he had liked that she had clung to him that way, relying on him being beside her. Even if he knew without a shadow of a doubt that the independent Shannon he knew would soon step up.

Fairly soon her smile and her wit had people stealing her from his side to introduce her to other beautiful people or to talk to like-minded supporters of community projects.

She was a hit.

Connor wouldn't have expected anything less.

Finally extricating himself from a group who had been most eager to bend the ear of the new owner of Devenish Enterprises, he stood to one side of the room to watch her.

She really was beautiful. The dress had caught his eye in a shop window when he had been stuck in traffic going to an early meeting. The exact green of her eyes when she was aroused, he had known instinctively it would look stunning on her. But it took her to be wearing it for the dress to take on a whole new dimension.

With her back to him, the halter neck afforded him a mesmerizing view of creamy skin from her shoulders to the slight inward curve above the base of her spine and with her hair up he couldn't help watching the way her long elegant neck turned, how the movement of her head as she talked would frequently offer up that sensitive section of skin below her ear that he loved so much.

And his body tightened in response to the thought of running his tongue along that skin, just so she would make those little sighs she made.

Her head turned, her large glittering eyes searching the room until she found him. And when she smiled, for the first time in his life Connor understood what people meant when they talked about someone being the only one they could see in a crowded room.

Someone sought her attention again, drawing her down the room so that Connor got to watch the long skirt shimmer around her legs as she moved. He wondered how it felt against her skin, how she felt with it against her skin. He even took a deep breath as he debated what she was wearing underneath it that was so invisible to the naked eye—and decided there and then that they had stayed as long as they needed to.

But before he could stalk over to reclaim her he noticed the group she was being introduced to—some of their faces *very* familiar to him. And he smiled a knowing smile. All right, he could wait. Once she'd finished talking to them, *she'd* come to him.

'Connor.'

'What the hell are you doing here?'

His younger brother walked straight over and embraced him in a manly, back-slapping, brief hug, before standing back and grinning at him. 'Hottest ticket in town? Where else would I be?'

Connor laughed. 'You might have mentioned you were coming when I saw you at the weekend.'

'You never asked.'

Connor shook his head, a broad grin on his face. 'I take it there's a woman involved in your decision to be here.'

And Mal laughed in return. 'You know me.'

'How did I guess?' Connor smiled.

Then Mal's expression changed and he took a deep breath before lowering his voice. 'Mum rang today.'

Connor sighed impatiently. 'I thought we agreed to leave me be on this. *Remember?* Just about ten minutes before we went jumping off a mountain at the crack of dawn on Saturday?'

'She really wants to see you.'

Feeling the familiar dark cloud descending above his head, Connor automatically sought Shannon across the room, watching as she laughed, her hand lifting to brush an invisible lock of hair behind her ear. And he could almost hear her voice in his ear telling him in no uncertain terms just what she thought of him not talking to his mother—which made him smile wryly.

'I'll go see her next week.'

'You will?' His brother's expression of disbelief told the tale of how unexpected Connor's answer was. 'Just like that? When half the family has been trying to speak to you for weeks and you haven't been answering their calls?'

Connor shot him a warning glance. 'And I told each and

every one of them that if they'd had the same bombshell dropped on them I did then they'd have needed some space too. Remember that bit?'

'Well, yeah, but this is the family we're chatting about here. They were never going to leave it be, you know that. You'd have been the same if it had been one of us.'

Yes, he would. But he doubted any of the rest of them would have taken the news the same way he had. If he hadn't already been so unsettled, so jealous of his older brother's happiness, so desperate to get away from the responsibility he had unwillingly shouldered for years, then maybe he wouldn't have felt that discovering he wasn't a full member of the family was some kind of retribution for not appreciating what he'd already had.

Blaming his mother for something that had happened before he was born wasn't going to fix what had already been wrong with him, was it?

Mal wasn't done. 'You need to speak to Rory too.'

Connor could feel any semblance of the good mood he'd had trickling away like water through his fingers. 'Rory knows where to find me.'

'I don't think he thinks it's his job to come to you.'

'Well, he can think what he wants.'

'You two are too alike, that's the problem. If you'd just both—'

Connor fixed him with a steely stare, his mouth a thin line. 'Well, you see, that's where you'd be wrong. We're nothing alike.'

'Mal?'

Connor frowned hard as he watched Shannon smile broadly at the younger man—who gaped at her in return. 'Shannon? No way! Wow, girl—you look fantastic!'

She leaned in closer to inform him, 'That's your brother's doing—he bought the dress.'

He gaped all the more at Connor. *'Did he now?'*

There was no way Connor was going to stand there and let his brother look at him with that knowing look. Hell, no. Already a grin was growing that, if he knew Mal, would be followed by at least an hour's worth of ribbing…

'We're leaving now. Good to see you, Mal.'

Shannon frowned up at him. 'What if I don't want to leave?'

'You didn't want to come in not two hours ago.'

She tilted her head to the side, which left the exposed part of neck Connor had been appreciating not five minutes ago exposed to Mal's sweeping gaze. 'Maybe I changed my mind. Women do that.'

Connor scowled hard as Mal looked down past her neck. *'Mal—'* the warning tone was enough to get his attention '—has a date of his own somewhere to attend to.'

'Maybe I'd like to meet her.'

Oh, he knew that edge to her voice. Only too well. When she said the words so calmly and so carefully, it meant they were two steps away from yet another argument. And there was no way he was letting that happen where they were. Or in front of his kid brother.

Which left him the option of standing there to make nice long enough for Mal to tell her all about the bust-up he'd had with Rory or dragging her back home where he could deal with the fallout the way he knew worked best.

He chose the latter. 'You don't want to keep Mal away from enjoying the rest of the kind of evening he no doubt has planned with her any more than he would want to keep us from the same, do you?'

Mal made a grimace, stepping back a little as they faced off against each other. 'Well, good to see that you two picked up exactly where you left off in the whole battle-of-wills thing. Let me know who survives.'

Shannon smiled sweetly at him. 'It was nice to see you Mal.'

'You too, Shannon. We've missed you.' He grinned over at Connor as he stepped away. 'We used to talk about you a lot after you left.'

Next time Connor saw his kid brother he would pay for that.

But he had another storm to weather first as Shannon stepped closer to him, smiling through gritted teeth at someone she must have met earlier as they passed by, before she turned her head to tell him, 'And now we really are leaving. Before I ruin any good impression I may have made on anyone I met tonight by telling you exactly what I think of you right this very second.'

When they were in the car she gave him the silent treatment while she tried to get her anger under control enough to speak.

And he seemed content to let the silence continue, which probably meant he thought he could find a way out of this one. Well, he could think again!

Because there was no way he could be such a complete ass and then think that sex would solve everything.

'You spoke to McIlwaine and Murphy, I saw.'

Shannon shook her head, her tongue shoved firmly into the corner of her cheek as she stared ahead. 'Who?'

'The men who want to build the shopping mall where your building sits.'

She turned her head so fast that she almost put her neck out. 'You're going to try and get round what you just did by playing the "I done good" card? Oh, you're a piece of work!'

'They told you about your building.'

'Well, as a matter of fact, yes, they did.' She forgot about her dress and folded her arms firmly across her breasts. 'They even asked me to try and persuade you to reconsider. Seems it has put quite a spanner in their plan, you backing out of the sale.'

'Picked the wrong woman to persuade, didn't they?'

'Well, why *wouldn't* they think I could persuade you? I mean, that's how it's done in some places, isn't it? Business deals done over the pillow, so to speak.'

He slammed on the brakes so hard at the junction that they were both thrown forward a little in their seats, Connor's face livid with anger when he looked at her. 'They *said* that to you?'

'No—' her mouth curved into a smirk '—but if they had it wouldn't have been any worse than what you just said to your brother about leaving to have sex. That doesn't make me seem at all *easy* to you?'

'I didn't say that to Mal!'

'You may as well have done!' She was really getting into her stride now. 'What else was he going to think you meant? You just threw that out there to get to leave—so you could stop me from talking to him—because if *you're* not talking to your family, then *I* shouldn't either, right?'

'It didn't occur to you that maybe I might not want you dragged into that?'

'O-h-h.' She laughed incredulously, 'I more than get where I stand in the great scheme of things with you—don't you worry.'

'And what does *that* mean?'

'It doesn't matter what it means.' The truth of that hit her like a slap in the face. Because it was true, wasn't it? No matter how many times she argued with Connor, he always seemed to manage to take control. Whether that was done by bully tactics, doing something amazingly nice to try and negate it, or just simply by trying to make it all better for a while by having sex. He was controlling her life. And he could do it because a part of her still probably loved him. She'd known that the minute McIlwaine and Murphy had told her he'd backed out of the sale. When, for a brief second, she had wanted to run across and kiss him silly because she'd been so happy.

Only to have him tell his brother they were off to have sex.

In *his* mind he probably saw it as his reward for doing the right thing—when he could have done the right thing to begin with, and she wouldn't have been left feeling as if it was just another move in whatever game he was playing with her.

'So long as you get to do everything on your terms then everything is fine, isn't it?' she said.

She turned her face away, looking out of the side window as they got close to home. Because she'd be damned before he would see the angry tears that were forming in the backs of her eyes.

Behind her, she heard the hiss as he forced out a swear word, the gear stick being yanked violently into place. 'I have *no* idea how your mind works sometimes.'

'You don't want to know.' The words were flat, emotionless, but that was what she did when she was hurting most, wasn't it? She shut herself off. Closed down inside. It was a survival tactic she had learnt the hard way.

Connor didn't say anything in reply for a long while, the tension inside the car palpable until, as they made the last turn onto the cobbled street, he took a breath and answered her in a similarly flat tone.

'You see, that's where you're wrong. I do want to know. I want to know every thought you have, I want to hear your opinions—even when I don't agree with them. I want you to yell at me when you're mad and laugh when you're happy. Because when you shut yourself off—that's when we have the most trouble. And if this is going to stand any chance of working, then we need to find a way around that.'

The car came to a halt in the same space it had occupied when he'd first arrived. But when Shannon reached for her seat-belt release, he captured her hand and held it tight, stopping her from escaping while she fought hard against the tears that were so determined to break free.

'We need to talk whatever this is through.'

She swallowed hard. 'I don't want to talk.'

'Than how are we supposed to fix this?'

'We're not.'

He let go of her hand. 'So what, then? Now that you know you have your building safe you don't have to make an effort any more? Or is it that now you've not got that to hide behind you might actually have to open up?'

That got her to look at him—her glare scathing.

'Because that's what the real problem is, isn't it?'

'Well, you're obviously the expert here. So well done. Congratulations. Whatever game you're playing, you win.'

When she got out of the car, slamming the door behind her, she let an angry sob out, fumbling in her small clutch bag to find her keys while she looked down at it through eyes threatening tears.

At the door she couldn't get the key in and as she sniffed loudly his hand appeared—taking the key from her. He didn't say a word, just leaned past her to fit it and turn it, while

Shannon stared downwards, the first tears balancing precariously on her lashes.

He pushed the door open. Stood back.

And Shannon walked through, opened the second door, leaning in to flick the light switch. Then, swallowing down the knot sitting at the base of her throat, she looked over her shoulder.

'I'm sorry, Connor. I can't do this with you any more. I thought I could, but I can't.'

'Can't do what?' He stepped in through the outer door, his dark eyes focused completely on her.

She swallowed again. 'This. Us. Whatever *this is—I* can't do it any more.'

'Because it hurts too much to try?'

Her breath caught, but when she tried she couldn't get the words out. So she nodded, just the once. Before looking away, and walking further into the foyer—turning around when she was in the centre, her hands on her hips, head tilted back to look up at the peeling paint on the cornice while she fought for some semblance of control.

She should never, *ever,* have conned herself into believing she could do this again.

What was she? Masochistic? So desperately in need of punishment for something she had long since paid for?

Connor walked to her with silent steps, stopping a 'safe' distance from her, as if he knew to come closer would only make things worse. He even seemed to understand that she needed a minute, that once she had that minute she might maybe tell him more to help him understand.

She took a breath, shaking her head with fresh determination. 'It's not enough.'

His deep voice remained low. 'What isn't?'

'This—' She exhaled the word, her arm swinging out to her side as she finally looked at him again. 'This fighting and then trying to fix it with sex.'

'And you think that's all we do?'

'It's what we *did!*'

His dark brows quirked. 'Wow.'

Shannon watched as his hand rose to run back through his hair. Then he looked her in the eye again, his voice still low.

'I don't think that was all we did.'

His calm response made her even angrier. 'Well, it was how it felt.'

'During or after?'

The question made her avoid his steady gaze, because even telling him as much as she had was costing her.

'I'm not saying that the act itself wasn't—'

'Well, at least we agree on that—that's a start. But in some way I've left you feeling used? Is that what you're saying?'

'No!' She frowned hard at his interpretation. 'It's not that either. What we did—we did together. And I wanted it—I did. But it just felt—'

'Like a one-night stand—sex for sex's sake—like there was nothing there except the release of sexual tension?' He shrugged his shoulders. 'Help me out here.'

Although a part of her understood that the change of tone in his voice was more to do with frustration and confusion than with any anger on his behalf—the very fact that he had worded it the way he had was enough to put her back up again. As if it confirmed to her that he had known that was exactly what it had been. Which made her right, didn't it?

And maybe that was what she needed. Maybe she needed

him to confirm it for her to get her to hate him again. To make her angry enough to finally send him away.

'It *was* sex, Connor. *That's all.* And I'm sorry, but that's just not enough for me. I need more than that.' She shrugged her shoulders, feigning nonchalance. 'And the truth is, I just don't think you have it in you to give me more. So, we're done.'

It was a low blow. And it was the first time in her life she had ever seen Connor look lost for words. But his recovery was quick, any hint of confusion or frustration—or even the patience he had shown so far—immediately replaced with out and out anger. So that she was left in no doubt she had just hit the mark.

'Is that the game we're playing now? Do I even *know* you?' He shook his head. 'Any wonder you're still on your own if this is how you deal with the beginning of a relationship! All of this is nothing but sex to you? You think we do this constant battle of wills for no reason? You seem to forget that we had years of history before we even got started this time round! But then walking away is your thing, isn't it? It's what you do best.' He laughed cruelly. '*Man,* and you think *I'm* messed up inside!'

Rather than backing down in the face of such raw anger she met fire with fire, her voice rising to echo around the large space.

'And you seem to forget that we spent seven years *apart!* You think that you're the only one who went through some kind of emotional upheaval in that time, Connor? You think that just because I argue with you and challenge the things you do that that means I'm the one with all the great answers to life's problems? Well, I'm *not!*' She jerked a pointed finger at the ground. 'I have just as much to deal with from those seven years as you do! *Probably more.* Because you always breezed through life and nothing was difficult for you until the day you found out you had a different father from the man who raised you. You have *no* idea what *I* might have gone through!'

'And just how am I *supposed to* when you keep fighting me off?'

Stunned into silence by how much she had just let out, she stood frozen to the spot, her breathing as rapid as the erratic beating of her heart. She stared at Connor with wide eyes, watching as he waged the same inner battle with himself to gain control.

It would have been so very easy to close the distance between them and give in to a raging passion to dissipate the tension again. But that was what had started this in the first place, wasn't it?

And she just couldn't keep on doing it.

Connor moved before she did, both hands lifting to rub up and down his face while he started pacing up and down in front of her. Then, side on, he nodded, as if he'd made some kind of decision, before he turned his head to look at her, one long finger waggling briefly in her direction.

'At least we're getting down to the crux of it now, aren't we?' The pointing stopped and the pacing continued. 'I knew there was *something.* It's been there since the first day. Don't get me wrong.' He glanced at her again with a wry smile. 'You're *good* at trying to cover it up behind the guts and quirkiness I'm used to. But I knew there was something different. Something that happened that changed you and left you hiding away in this place.'

The air in her lungs stilled on an inward gasp that she held onto. *Dear Lord.* What had she just done? Connor had never been dumb. And now she'd just given him some of the pieces of the puzzle, hadn't she?

He stopped pacing again while he thought, and then—so suddenly it made her jump—he stepped in front of her, less than a few feet separating them. 'You're right. Neither of us knows what the other went through in those seven years. There's no way we could. But you're wrong about me breezing through life, Shannon—I wish you weren't, but you are.'

She exhaled, took a deep, shaky breath. It had never in a million years occurred to her that he had been unhappy before he had found out about Frank McMahon. And it stunned her beyond belief.

Connor stepped another step closer, his voice husky. 'The only difference between us is that I'm not the one trying to turn tail and run away from this, *whatever it is.* So, fine, we both have stuff. Who doesn't? Big deal. What this needs is time. You've just got to decide that you're prepared to put in that time. And a good dose of old-fashioned trust.'

Could she really do that? How could she begin to tell him about the pain she carried when he was so tied up in that pain? By making it a mutual sharing he was inviting her to help him work through whatever it was he was carrying around—which made it a shared therapy, didn't it? And that made it so much harder for her not to at least give it a try.

Could she manage to get through it without falling for him twice as hard as she had the first time round? That would be the gamble she'd be taking.

But what if helping him work through all the things he was having difficulty dealing with now was her only way of making up for what she had held back from him?

While her heart demanded she try, her head kept weighing up the odds of an outcome that wouldn't cause both of them pain—and in the meantime Connor had stepped another step closer.

'Now with that out there in the open, let's move on to the sex issue. I'm assuming that we're looking at the age-old debate of sex versus making love are we?'

There were times when he really could read her mind, weren't there?

'Yes, I think we are.'

He nodded. 'Yeah, I thought so. C'mon, then—'

Shannon's eyes widened as he grasped her hand in his and tugged her towards the stairs, her voice rising again. 'Oh, no, you can't keep trying to solve it like *that!*'

Still tugging her, he threw the words over his shoulder. 'Well, it's getting solved somehow. And I, for one, am getting sick of pacing.'

'Connor, let go of me!' She practically careered into his back when he stopped suddenly, releasing her hand at the same time to turn round and hold his hands up in surrender.

'Fine—look—no hands. I'm serious, Shannon—I'm not leaving 'til this is resolved one way or another. Don't make me carry you up three flights.'

And Shannon knew he meant it. 'We're just talking.'

'I'll leave that decision to you. We'll talk it through, then, if it's what you want, I'll go.'

'You'll leave?'

Another nod. 'For tonight.'

When he held his hand out in silent invitation she stared at it for a long time. But who was she kidding? She knew she was going to go upstairs with him and talk it through. She'd already dug a deep enough hole.

But she'd feel better if she managed not to touch him just

yet, so she reached out and set her clutch bag in his open hand, glancing up into his eyes as he smiled in amusement. 'I hate you.'

'No, you don't. And that's the biggest problem you've got, if you bother being honest with yourself.'

CHAPTER ELEVEN

UP IN SHANNON'S apartment, Connor set the small bag she had handed him on the kitchen counter while he watched her move around the room, switching on table lamps that cast a soft glow around them.

She had said that she wanted more and that she didn't think he had more to give her.

That had grated on him more than anything ever had.

She sat down on one of the large sofas that dominated the living area, smoothing her hands down over the soft material of her long skirt as she took a breath and looked up at him.

'All right, then.'

The determined upward lift of her chin brought another smile to his mouth as he walked across to sit on the other sofa, facing her. But for a long while he didn't speak, he just smiled at her, until eventually she sighed and shook her head.

'I'm glad you find all this so amusing.'

'I don't.' He shrugged his shoulders, reaching up to undo his bow-tie and loosen the top button of his shirt. 'I just can't remember ever being on a first date when I ended up sitting down to have a conversation about the vagaries of sex. It's not exactly what I had planned for the evening.'

Her arched brows rose in challenge. 'Which pretty much brings us onto the subject of sex anyway, doesn't it?'

'And there you go differentiating between sex and making love again. When what you need to realize is that, with us, there isn't a difference.'

'Spoken like a man.'

'That's a whole other argument for another day, that one.'

'And that's what we do, isn't it? We argue. About pretty much everything.'

He leaned forwards, resting his elbows on his thighs, 'Yes. It's what we do. Lots of couples argue.'

There was a flicker of surprise in the green of her eyes. 'We're *a couple* now?'

'If we're not, then what are we?'

'And when did that happen in your mind? 'Cos I must have missed that memo.'

'Shannon, we've always been a couple—one way or another. This is just the first time we've had to deal with it, that's all.' He smiled again when she looked distinctly as if he'd just told her something that had never occurred to her before. 'Tell me this—when we slept together the first time, did that feel like just sex between two people seeking a cheap release to you?'

The direct question brought her gaze up to lock with his, her eyes softening briefly as she played the memory in her mind, so that he knew the answer before she said it.

'No. Now that I know you knew it was me I know that was us making love. But for your information, I wasn't playing a game. It was something I wanted and I figured if I made it an anonymous fantasy it might be something you'd want too.'

Connor's eyes widened slightly. 'Nice to know your low

opinion of me goes so far back. All right, then, so, what was different this time?'

And her brows quirked again, this time in disbelief. 'The fact that you have to even ask me tells me you're not going to understand the problem.'

'I was giving you the opportunity to tell me how you saw it. That's all. But if you want me to say what I think, then, fine—I'll tell you.' He looked to the side, away from her face, while he put the words together in his head first. It was getting to be a necessity around Shannon. 'I think the reason it has blown up out of all proportion in your mind is the word "sex." But you need to remember that the phrase "make-up sex" was yours, not mine.'

She opened her mouth to protest.

'No. I gave you the opportunity to go first and you didn't take it, so now I'm just telling you what I think. And then you can say what you think.'

The simple order did what any order or demand he dished out normally did with her. It put her back up. But he loved that she fought him on those issues. He was a strong-minded male, after all; it was the very fact that she was equally strong-willed that made them such a combustible combination.

So, while she straightened her spine, folded her arms across her breasts and lifted her chin another distinct notch, he kept right on going. 'It was a phrase, nothing more and I understood that—I thought you did too—'

The terse interruption surprised him. 'Yes, fine, you're right—I gave it that label and that label has stuck in my head ever since.'

Connor jumped on the opportunity. 'And can you tell me why?'

The fact that she struggled so long to find the words to answer him told him how difficult she was finding it to talk it through. 'Probably because you left so fast and didn't bother calling for three days. It made it feel like a one-night stand—which made it feel like sex for sex's sake. And that left me feeling…'

Connor leaned forward when her words tailed off. 'Feeling what?'

She swallowed hard, her gaze dropping down to study the toe of her shoe as she moved her foot from side to side. 'Empty, if you must know. Like I should never have let it happen again.'

The thought of her feeling that way almost floored him. Empty was such a huge feeling. He knew that. And never in a million years would he have wanted to leave her feeling like that. He'd always prided himself on the fact that any partner he had felt as fulfilled by the act as he did. It was the man's job. But somehow he had left her feeling used, tawdry, and that hadn't been what he'd been aiming for—not with Shannon, of all people.

She was worth so much more than that.

'I never meant for you to feel like that.'

Her lashes rose enough for her to look at him. 'I know. I guess I just stupidly thought I would get to hear your voice at some point over the weekend, that, I dunno—you might maybe have bothered to call to say hi or at least talk about the weather.'

'I thought you understood what I was doing this weekend.' He frowned a little. 'I told you I was away.'

She nodded. 'You said you were hang-gliding on Saturday with some of the staff from the gym.'

'No, well, yes. But it was a bit more than that. It was a

team-building weekend. They take us to the middle of nowhere and we camp out. And then we spend the weekend doing a mixture of challenges that make us work together—bridge-building, rock-climbing, hang-gliding. Every gym does it once a year to help them work together better.' He sighed, taking a moment as he tried to remember how much he had told her at the time. He had been sure he'd explained all that. 'And I'd signed up for this one a long time ago. I really thought I'd explained that. But what I maybe didn't explain is it's a wilderness type idea—so that means no laptops, no iPods—definitely no phones. They're very specific on that. And I didn't think you'd appreciate a call at one in the morning when I was driving back home, after leaving the last of the team who travelled with me.'

Shannon stared at him from beneath her lashes. 'You didn't tell me all of that.'

'I should have.'

'Yes, you should. It might have helped.'

He nodded, smiling a small smile when she didn't call him on it. Was he finally making some headway? Well, if forthright was what it took…. 'But I need to carry that through to today for you too, don't I?'

A smile twitched at the edges of her mouth.

'This morning I had company meetings—this afternoon too. Some of them put back from Friday so I could spend the day here.' He grimaced. 'I've had nothing but meetings for weeks now, as it happens, and I'm sick to death of them. But, yes, I could have called.'

Her eyes sparkled across at him. Oh, she knew she had him on this, didn't she? He'd messed up. His arrogance had let him assume that she'd have no problem with him disappearing for a few days because she'd known he was coming back. He'd assumed she'd known that meant he wasn't bailing on her and that there wasn't a problem with him *wanting* to come back. But that was what assuming got him. Some consideration would have worked a lot better.

'That was obviously a mistake too. But now that I know it's a problem I can make damn sure it's not a problem again. If I have an early meeting I'll call you at six when I get up—and if I'm coming back from somewhere, even if it's three in the morning, I'll call. And that'll fix it, will it?'

He knew she'd never go for that either. She wasn't the type to try keeping someone on a leash…

And, right enough, her smile grew. 'Let's just not go to the opposite extreme either. There's bound to be a compromise in there somewhere.'

If she was open to discussing compromises, then he was making ground, wasn't he? That left him with just the one hurdle to get past so he could breathe again.

'All right. That leaves us with the sex versus making love again.'

Her smile faded. Lifting her chin again, she frowned as she glanced around the room—giving the distinct impression of someone seeking an escape, which brought an affectionate smile to Connor's face that he didn't try to hide from her.

She chanced a glance at him from the corner of her eye. Saw the smile.

And Connor waited while she battled with herself over whether to listen or to argue again and try to run. She could *try* the latter. But she wouldn't get far.

Shannon sighed.

Well, she'd asked for this, hadn't she?

Thing was, piece by piece and subject by subject, Connor was taking the time to ease her through all of the things that worried her. And surely he wouldn't do that if it didn't matter to him a little?

If she'd had the courage downstairs to tell him that the 'not enough' she had been referring to had more to do with the lack of real emotion then she could probably have avoided all of this. Because that was the real truth behind her emptiness, wasn't it? She had wanted the whole package from him once before and hadn't got it. It was what she had meant when she had said she didn't think he had it in him to give. She had prior experience.

Not that she thought he was incapable of love. She just didn't believe he was capable of loving her the way she would want him to. But she had always known that. Right from the start. Both times.

When she turned her face fully towards him, she studied him for a long while—searching his eyes for some sign that this wasn't just damage control for him. That it could really matter.

And there was such a fierce warmth in his dark eyes that she was almost rocked back by the force of it.

It was genuine affection she could see, affection for *her*. And when he spoke, his voice wasn't just low and deep. There was an edge to it that went straight from her ears to her heart, and, almost as if her heart hoped for its meaning before her mind could accept there was even a chance of it, it leapt, and sped up in response.

'The only difference I can see between the first time we were together and this time is that the first time was the slow and torturous kind of love-making and this time was the hot and fast kind. And I think it's maybe the slow and torturous that works best for you.'

Shannon swallowed hard.

'For a while, anyway, until you trust me enough to play a little.' His smile took on a purely sexual edge. 'You need to remove the word "sex" from your mind when it refers to what we do, Shannon. We don't just have sex. We know each other too well for that.'

Even listening to him talking about it—while he looked at her with that warmth in his eyes, and that wicked smile on his face—it *felt* as if he were already beginning to make love to her, all over again.

'Mal said that we had picked up where we left off—and he was right. That's exactly what we've done. The only difference is we've had more baggage in the way this time round. So, yes, we've fought more—but the outcome has been exactly the same, hasn't it? Whether we've approached it from a friendship angle or from an antagonistic angle, we always end up back at the same place.'

Did that mean that he knew how much she had loved him before? Did it mean that he knew a part of her had never stopped loving him? It was certainly the reason why she'd been having so much difficulty with all of it lately, wasn't it?

'This…chemistry…we have—it's always been there. I don't think that something on so basic a level is something that anyone has any control over. It's here now. You can feel it just as much as I can.'

Yes, she could. Connor had once talked about the building being a pink elephant constantly between them—if that was the case then between them now was an open fire, the heat from the flames fanning out to wash over her skin.

Thick dark lashes blinked slowly as he studied her with an intensity that took her breath away all over again. 'And I know you can feel it. Because I *know* you. Right now it's in your eyes—they go a darker shade of green when you're turned on. Did you know that?'

Shannon slowly shook her head.

Connor nodded in reply. 'They do. It's why I knew that dress would look so spectacular on you. It's the same shade your eyes are right now.'

She ran her tongue over her lips.

And his smile grew as he looked at her mouth. 'You do that too. You wet your lips just like that—which, whether you know it or not, is an invitation for me to kiss you. It's like you're getting your mouth ready for me. And for the record, it's one of the things I find sexiest about you. *One* of the things...'

Shannon was slowly reaching boiling point, her lips parted as she drew in deeper, faster breaths of the heated, heavy air that hung between them. He hadn't even touched her and she was so aroused that she dearly wanted to squirm on the soft cushions beneath her to relieve some of the ache between her legs.

His smouldering gaze dropped lower, following the line of her neck to the deep vee at the front of her dress, his voice taking on a husky edge that left her in no doubt that he was as turned on as she was.

'Though the way your breathing changes is damn sexy too. Deeper breaths, like you're taking now—that get faster and shorter when you're close to the point where you can't take any more.'

'Connor—' His name came out on a hoarse, agonized whisper—because she really *couldn't* take any more.

The sound brought his gaze back to her eyes. 'I know you

want me. And you know me well enough to look at me right now and know that I want you too. This is always here with us—it's when we fight it that we end up arguing the most. But never, ever, for one second, think that it hasn't always been here. This isn't just sex, Shannon—it's much, much more than that.'

Shannon knew he was right. For the first time in a long time she had no desire to argue with him over it—because there was really no point in trying to deny any of it. Everything he had said about the signals she sent out was true. Looking at him, she could see the signals in him too—the intense heat of his gaze, the slight part of his sensual mouth, the exaggerated rise and fall of his chest beneath his crisp white shirt, and—when her gaze dared to drop lower to his wide-spread legs—the ridge of his erection pressed against his stretched trousers.

'Shannon—' Her name was spoken on a warning tone, bringing her gaze back up to his face.

And the set of his jaw, the tight line of his mouth, the hooded eyes told her volumes about his state of arousal. Yes, she could read the signs too. Because she knew him every bit as well as he knew her in that department.

She tilted her head, looking at him with the kind of confidently slow, seductive smile a woman gave when she knew she had equal powers of attraction to her man as he did to her. Then, purposefully, she licked her lips to show him what she wanted him to do while she leaned forwards, perched on the edge of the sofa.

'You said I could decide whether you stayed or left.'

He leaned forwards, balancing on the edge of the sofa he was on. 'Yes, I did. But I also said I would be back. I'm not going away, Shannon, no matter how many times you try to push me away. Get that clear. So, whether we clear this up today, tomorrow, or next week, it's getting cleared up. Make no mistake about that.'

And Shannon knew, even now, when they were both so aroused that if she said go, he would. He was a man of his word. And he would see it as another way to earn her trust. But she didn't need him to leave and keep coming back to earn her trust. It had never been a trust issue.

She didn't need him to prove himself to her. What she needed was to take a chance—to meet him halfway, to work through the pain that seven years apart from him had brought her way, and to hope and pray that they could build something strong enough to survive when she told him the truth.

'Stay.'

The slow exhalation was immediately followed by an expression that almost looked like relief. Then he smiled at her with that oh-so-sexy smile she loved so much while he told her, 'Just so you know—this time is the slow and torturous version of the love-making we do. And I'm talking *very* slow. And *extremely* torturous.'

Shannon's eyes closed briefly as the ecstasy of anticipation caused her body to flood all over again. 'It's already torturous.'

But he didn't move, not yet—almost as if he was loath to stop her from suffering. And just when she was about to take matters into her own hands—literally—his dark brows quirked in question. 'Do we have a bedroom this time?'

She lifted her arm to point to her left.

And it was then that he stood up, his hand offered to her, palm upwards, the same way it had been at the foot of the stairs.

So Shannon reached her hand out and placed it in his, her fingers tangling with his while she watched. Such a small gesture, so much meaning. With her paler, smaller hand framed by his larger, tanned hand she was telling him that she trusted him, that, in a small way, she was surrendering herself to what came next.

Her eyes rose, head tilting right back so she could look into his eyes as he drew her to her feet. And with their gazes locked, he lifted the back of her hand to his mouth, his lips warm against her skin, his breath fanning over the back of her wrist.

And Shannon had *thought* she had loved him before…

CHAPTER TWELVE

'DON'T MOVE.'

The soft demand was made as Connor stood Shannon at the side of the bed, her back close to the dressing table. So she stood still while he found the nearest lamp and stepped past her to close the bedroom door. Then he was back in front of her, his gaze once again fixed on hers.

It slid to the side, his head tilting closer to her face, forwards to look behind her ear, so that his warm breath was on the side of her neck and the scent of his aftershave filled her nostrils

Large hands slowly rose to the droplet earring brushing the skin below her earlobe and he focused on removing the clasp at the back to free it from her ear, his gaze returning briefly to hers as he completed the task and set the earring down on the dresser.

And Shannon's heart twisted at the simple tenderness of it, her neck tilting to the other side, eyelids heavy, as his attention moved to her other ear—repeating the action.

And his gaze locked with hers again while she stared back up at him.

Then his fingertips brushed from her bare shoulders, down

each of her arms, until he touched the bracelet on one wrist and lifted the arm to carefully remove it. Setting it silently onto the dresser before his gaze came back to lock with hers.

And still he didn't speak. He didn't have to. Because, as his attention went to the pendant lying at the base of her throat, his gaze following the line of the chain until he had to tilt his head over one bare shoulder to unhook the tiny clasp, he was saying more *without* words—his gentleness and careful focus on each task touching her deep inside her soul in the same way that he had when he had first made love to her.

He let the pendant slide down a little between her breasts, watching the reaction in her eyes before it too joined the other items on the dresser. Then his hands lifted again, fingertips brushing along each side of her neck, teasing the sensitive nerve endings awake as he searched up into the intricate knot of her hair for the clips that held it in place.

Shannon closed her eyes as he drew each one free, her weight swaying forwards off her high heels as she tried to compensate for her wobbling knees. As the last clip was placed on the dresser, she opened her eyes, knowing before she did that he would be looking at her as his fingers drew her hair down around her face and over her shoulders.

'Shake it loose for me.' He stepped back a little to watch as she tossed her head from side to side.

Confidence growing exponentially by the second, she smiled as her hair fell around her face, Connor seeming to revel simply in watching her.

Using his hands on her shoulders to turn her around, so that she could see the two of them reflected in the mirror above the dresser, he continued smiling as he watched her expression change, her eyes wide with wonder at the sight of her hair cascading in unfamiliar soft waves around her face, rising to look at the flush on her cheeks, before they rose further and locked with his.

'I don't think you know how beautiful you are.' He smoothed her hair back, running his fingers down through the long silky length until he was tracing the rise and fall of the ridges of her spine, which made Shannon arch her back, her head falling back against his shoulder. 'You always were.'

Not that it wasn't what she wanted to hear, but, 'No, I wasn't. Don't you remember? I had braces for years.'

'No, I don't remember that. And you're trying to ruin a compliment that I'm not taking back.'

She nodded her head up and down against his jacket. 'I did, though—from fifteen to seventeen.'

'Ah.' He nodded, turning his head to press a kiss against her hair. 'The shy and quiet years. You see, you weren't a pain in the ass until you turned eighteen.'

Shannon nudged him with her elbow.

But even though he chuckled, he was already moving his hands up her spine, turning his fingers to brush the backs of his hands over her shoulder blades, pushing her forwards an inch or two so he could tilt her head forwards, smooth the hair from her neck and undo the tiny hooks of the dress's halter-neck.

The soft material slid down over her breasts in a whisper, leaving her staring at her reflection as his hands smoothed round to flatten over her ribcage, fingers splaying, his eyes fixed on hers in the mirror.

Shannon laid her head back again, tearing her gaze from his, so that they were both watching as his hands rose, cupping her breasts with such tenderness.

How could anyone blame her for wanting this?

But as his fingers moved, teasing her nipples into hard buds, she moaned, her lips parting to gasp in air—because it was almost *too* slow, too torturous to stand.

And Connor knew what he was doing to her, his head turning so that he had access to her neck—his lips leaving a string of butterfly-soft kisses on her skin before he whispered in her ear, 'And just think, we haven't even got started yet.'

She moaned in frustration. Then in annoyance as he freed her breasts and set her away from him again. But she should have known he wasn't stopping. So when she felt his fingers against the skin of her lower back and heard the soft hiss of the zip being lowered, she pursed her lips together, her gaze rising to watch his reaction as the dress slid to the floor and she stepped out of it, turning to face him.

Connor's face changed, a look of the same torture she had been feeling written all over him. When she tilted her head, her hair falling over one side of her face, one hip tilted towards him, he frowned, stifling a low groan as he looked up into her eyes.

'I've spent half of the night wondering what you were wearing under that dress that was so invisible.'

'I have a thing about nice underwear.' She glanced down at the sheer lace thong, stay-up stockings with their equally lacy top, and her ridiculously impractical strappy heels. 'And shoes. Shoes are my weakness.'

When she looked up, Connor was swallowing hard, his eyes a midnight black. 'Don't ever, *ever* lose either of those weaknesses. In fact. The stockings and the shoes can stay on. *Seriously.*'

No one had ever told her that to have a man like Connor so very visibly weak at the knees was such a huge turn-on. Someone so strong in body and in character hanging by a thread because he wanted her that badly—and she could see that in his eyes, in the clench of his jaw, the single, tiny bead of sweat that trailed down along the side of his gorgeous face.

She'd never felt so close to him before. They were truly equal in their weakness for each other.

'So, this torturous thing—that's supposed to be a one-way deal, is it?'

His dark eyes widened briefly at the question, his voice a low grumble. 'Sweetheart, if you don't think I'm tortured over here then you have no idea of how you look right now wearing what you're wearing.'

'Well, then…' she stepped closer, looking up at him from beneath long lashes '…shouldn't you be wearing less?'

Connor held his arms out to his sides. 'Be my guest.'

With another smile, she focused on pushing his jacket off his broad shoulders, Connor lowering his arms to help her out. Then she turned her attention to the small pearl buttons on his shirt, purposefully taking her time slipping each one free.

'Not that there isn't something incredibly sexy about a man in a dress shirt with a bow-tie loose around his neck. Many a fantasy has been launched on that image.'

'You just let me know what your fantasies are and I promise to do my very best to oblige…'

Her fingers still working on the buttons, she looked upwards, biting down on her lip as she thought. 'Mmm…'

Connor groaned again, the sound a low rumble in the base of his throat. 'Don't do that.'

Shannon blinked innocently at him. 'Do what?'

'Make that noise while you bite down on your lip.'

'Why?' She smiled mischievously. 'What's that a sign of? You're the one that knows me so well.'

'It's not a sign of anything,' He leaned in and suckled on the side of her neck again, his voice muffled against her skin. 'It's what you do when you come. Remind me and I'll let you know when you're doing it again, which incidentally…' his head rose as she undid the final button, her knuckles grazing against the flat skin above his trousers '…I intend making you do again and again tonight.'

Shannon's hands flattened out against his abdomen, smoothing up, fingers tracing over each of his ribs, while she revelled in the sensation of warm skin over tight muscle. 'All those years in the gym business stood you in good stead, didn't they?'

He grinned proudly as she slid the shirt off him, 'Very important to create the right impression for the clients, I feel.'

'Very.' She nodded in agreement, her hands already on the button of his trousers as she smiled again. 'I'm not the only beautiful one in the room.'

A look of chagrin was aimed her way. 'Men aren't beautiful.'

'This one is.' With the zip undone she slid the palms of her hands under the waistband and the edge of his underwear, bending her knees as she slid them both down his legs, her eyes full of what was hers to take. She could torture him to a whole other level if she—

'Shannon, don't even think about it.' He reached down, hands under her arms to pull her back upright. 'I meant it when I said I was tortured already. You do that and it'll take me at least a half hour to recover enough to do what I plan on doing.'

She chuckled. And he chuckled back in return, crushing her to him as he spun them in a circle to the edge of the bed. 'You're a witch.'

'Not with anyone else, I'm not.'

They stopped with the back of her knees against the mattress, Connor's expression and tone fierce as she swiped her hair out of her eyes.

'*Never* with anyone else. Ever again.'

'Connor—'

It was too much. And the fear of a promise made that might not be kept must have sounded in her voice, because he silenced her with a, 'Shh…'

And finally, for the first time in what felt like for ever, his mouth came down on hers in a heated kiss, placing a seal on his possessive words. He stole the air from her lungs, traced the parting of her lips with his tongue, until her mouth opened on a moaning sigh and she met him touch for touch, taste for taste, her hands rising to frame the strong lines of his face, her fingers threading back into his hair to draw him even closer.

But it still wasn't close enough. She wanted him as close as a man could be to a woman. She wanted him to fill her body, to take away any semblance of the emptiness she had felt without him for the last three days.

With his strong arms wrapped around her slender frame, he lowered her to the bed with a reverence that belied the ravage of his tongue inside her mouth.

He encouraged her without words to move further up the mattress, by using his arms to lift her a little, by then moving his hands down to the backs of her knees to lift her legs one by one as he removed her thong—her high heels pressed against the edge of the bed when he threw it over his shoulder. Then, with a long groan, he tore his mouth from hers.

'Back in a minute.'

Shannon rose onto her elbows to watch with amusement as he sought out his discarded jacket, retrieving the small box that he then ripped open—tossing it on the bed near her when he had what he sought. And Shannon turned to find it, lifting it to look up at him in challenge while she waved it back and forth.

'You only brought *three?*'

'A bumper pack would have been seen under my jacket.' He grinned at her. 'Don't worry, I can be creative.'

Then he was over her again, balancing on his elbows as he framed her face, his thumbs teasing the corners of her mouth. 'Now, where were we?'

Shannon framed his face in return, her eyes gleaming up at him as she ran her tongue over her lips and drew his head down. 'Right here.'

The kiss was slower, softer, warming her heart in places that had been so badly hurt in the past that she had closed them off so she wouldn't feel anything there ever again.

She bent her knees more, making a cradle for him to rest in as she wrapped her calves around his, creating static where her stockings brushed against the hair on his legs. And still they kissed, Connor's head lifting only long enough for him to kiss her from another angle while he pressed the tip of his erection against her slick heat.

Shannon writhed beneath him, her breathing rapid and shallow, her hips rising to meet him, inviting him deeper, pleading silently for him to end the torture.

When he slid his full length into her she wrenched her mouth from his, her head arched back into the covers as she gasped his name, his mouth on her jaw, on her neck, his teeth nipping against her collarbone. And all the while he was starting a slow rocking of his hips, building the knot of tension inside Shannon until she thought she might die if she didn't find a release soon.

'Connor—' She gasped his name again, looking up into his face as he rose above her on arms that shook as he tried to hold himself in check—his chest grazing back and forth so that her over-sensitized breasts were teased by coarse chest hair, creating a delicious friction that sent her closer and closer to the edge. *'Connor!'*

The constant gasping of his name and the little sighs and moans that she made seemed to drive him equally close to the edge, the struggle evident on his face and beneath her hands as she grasped at the taut muscles of his upper arms while he increased the rhythm, pushing into her a little harder with each stroke.

And when she began to buck beneath him in the throes of pleasure, her teeth biting down firmly on her bottom lip, he smiled briefly, then his body went rigid and a long, low groan of satisfaction pierced the air as he rested his forehead against hers.

Shannon looked up at his closed eyes, her body still trembling as the last ripples of intense pleasure spread out from her abdomen into every nerve ending of her body. She listened to their matched heavy breathing, felt the hard beat of his heart pressed against her own. And the overwhelming sense of love she felt for him was so complete that she just wanted to stay where they were for ever. To freeze the moment, to never have to visit a place where they weren't this close.

But there would be a day of reckoning, wouldn't there?

No matter if they managed to work everything else out, no matter how happy they were together—the day would come. It was just the way it was.

When he opened his eyes, he did it slowly, so that she had time to force the telltale pain from her eyes, instead smiling up at him with the smile of a woman who had just been taken to heaven and back.

'Well, hello, there. How you doin'?'

He grinned down at her. 'Not too shabby, as it happens. And I don't need to ask you—you're pretty vocal. Not that I'm complaining about that.'

Shannon giggled—an amazing sound to both of them—as she remembered how long it had been since she had last giggled that way and Connor pulled her on it by scowling ridiculously.

'Oh, there's something amusing is there?'

'Only that I'm still wearing my stockings and shoes.'

'And rightly so too.' He took a long moment to kiss her, his mouth then peppering small kisses over her cheeks, her eyelids, her forehead, then back to her mouth. 'So, which side of the bed do you want?'

The thought of spending a night wrapped in his arms almost brought tears to her eyes. This time she wasn't going to sneak away while he slept and he wasn't going to leave her on her own. *Bliss.*

'I want whatever side of it you're on.'

'I tend to sprawl in the middle—' he wriggled their still-joined bodies further up the bed '—and hog the duvet.'

'I believe that. But with a little training we might make you more considerate; given the time.'

When he looked down at her, his gaze was intense, his words deeply sincere. 'We have time.'

But no matter how she tried to convince herself that could be true, as Connor moved to remove her shoes and stockings before drawing her into his side she just knew that it wasn't. She was already on borrowed time.

CHAPTER THIRTEEN

MARIO BOUNDED INTO the end of the reading session as the last child was leaving. 'I tell ya. You can wait all day for a bus in this town and then two just roll in at the same time. It's always the way, isn't it?'

Shannon laughed at him. 'Have we had one too many coffees this morning, precious?'

He leaned in against her side. 'What is it with you and tall, dark and handsome men at the minute? Did you change your deodorant? 'Cos if you did, I might need to know what brand you're using…'

'What *are* you talking about you loon?'

Mario lowered his voice to a stage whisper. '*Well,* there's another *very* beautiful man in the foyer looking to talk to you. I told him you were spoken for but he still wants to see you…'

Shannon played along. 'Did he happen to say who he was?'

'He did. Just his first name, though…'

She smiled encouragingly. 'And do I get to know what that name is?'

'Rory. Suits him actually. Though I should warn you, this one is wearing a wedding ring.' He held his left hand up and tapped his ring finger. 'So even though you *are* spoken for, be careful. Don't get suckered in by a "my wife doesn't understand me" story...'

Connor smiled in satisfaction as he pushed open the inner door to find scaffolding half dismantled in the foyer. The work was almost done—which was just as well with the big party planned for that weekend.

It had taken nearly a solid twenty-four hours in bed to persuade Shannon that she should help him set up a community-owned trust to manage the place, even after he had tried playing the 'tax exempt to a charity' card. Not that he had in any way, shape, or form had a problem with the persuasion part. And it had been worth it to see her come alive with the project, her astute gaze never missing a trick with the building contractors who had worked wonders inside a few short weeks.

She even demonstrated her enthusiasm and rewarded him with another twenty-four hours. Connor officially loved Sundays now.

'Well, hello, lover.'

He grimaced at Mario's greeting. He wasn't sure he would ever adjust to a six-foot male who wore pink. No matter how much respect he had for the way Mario looked out for Shannon's welfare like some kind of loyal Great Dane.

'Hello, Mario. Where is she?'

'Who?'

Connor shook his head, smiling in resignation.

'Oh, you mean Shannon. She's upstairs. I'll lock up down here before I leave. Though I should warn you—I think she's ticked off at you. Just so you have a heads up.'

'Any idea what the builders did this time?'

'Don't think it was the builders.'

Well, it wasn't something *he'd* done, not this time. In fact, life had been fairly harmonious of late. He'd even been the perfect guy and looked after Shannon when she'd taken a stomach bug. Connor felt he was even more of a helluva guy than he'd been before he'd discovered her again.

So he held his hands up as he walked past the counter. 'Not me this time. I'm a guilt-free zone. Night, Mario.'

Mario laughed. 'G'night, Connor.'

Two steps away, a thought occurred to Connor, and he stepped backwards again. 'I have to ask you. Is your name really Mario?'

Mario rolled his eyes, leaning forwards to answer in a stage whisper, 'No telling.'

Connor answered with some trepidation. 'O-okay.'

Mario looked from side to side. 'It's Patrick. But Mario sounds much more interesting, don't you think?'

'Does Shannon know that?'

'No. So it's our secret.'

Connor laughed, taking the stairs two at a time to get to Shannon. Not pausing on any of the three flights, until he was standing in her doorway again, his eyes immediately searching the large room for her.

Norah Jones was singing in soft tones in the background, low light warming the room from an assortment of lamps and candles. And there, legs curled up beside her and a blanket over her knees, was Shannon.

Connor exhaled.

As if she had heard the sound, even over the music, her eyes rose and she blinked slowly as she studied him. And Connor could see the momentary caution there.

Uh-oh.

'Hello.'

He stepped into the room, his eyes still locked on her face as he got closer. 'Feeling better?'

'Yes, thanks.'

Stopping a few feet away from her, he narrowed his eyes as he searched the familiar green of hers. And there it was—the ever-elusive *something*. Only this time it was tinged with a something he knew only too well.

'What's wrong?'

Swinging the blanket back, she blinked up at him. 'Now, why would there be something wrong?'

'You see, that's why I'm asking. I have *no* idea. But Mario said I should be prepared before I came up here.' He leaned in for a brief kiss as she got close to him. Which she responded to the way she usually did, so he couldn't be in *that* much trouble.

But when he leaned back she was more blatant about blinking, her lashes fluttering as she accompanied it with an innocent pout. 'That's sweet that you two are such good friends now.' Then her head tilted and she smiled. 'Remind me to fire him again tomorrow…'

'You already fired him three times this week. I don't think he's going anywhere.'

'He *is* right, though. We do need to have another little one of our *talks.*'

'About what? 'Cos I know I haven't sold a building you love today, kicked any kittens or informed any small children that fairies don't exist. So it can't be me on your hit list.'

Shannon stepped round him and walked into the kitchen area of the large room, refilling her glass with water at the counter before she looked him directly in the eye again. 'Rory came to see me.'

Connor wouldn't have been any more surprised if she'd told him that Santa had been there. 'My brother came to see you to get *you* to talk to me? Oh, that's rich. Not like him to get a woman to do his dirty work.'

Shannon laughed sarcastically. 'From what I hear, you're damn lucky his wife didn't find you first.'

The thought of that raised the first open smile he'd smiled in a while when he thought about his elder brother. 'Well, I'll grant you, Cara can be scary when she gets on a roll. But it's not like Rory not to pick his own fights.'

'Oh, I think if he'd found you he'd have picked a fight all right. From what he tells me you two still have the odd wrestling match.' She shook her head. 'You'd think two grown men would have more sense.'

'It takes two to make a wrestling match. And he threw the first punch this time.' Connor scowled hard as he replayed that day in his mind. It had been ugly. 'Anyway, he shouldn't have to hide behind his wife, or you.'

When he folded his arms across his chest Shannon shook her head again. 'You're both pathetic.'

'So what did he want you to do exactly? Send me home to apologize to him with my tail between my legs?'

She ignored his sarcasm, sipping her water before she pursed her lips together in thought, her gaze focusing on the glass as she ran her forefinger around the rim. 'Don't you want to know why he didn't want his wife traipsing up here even when she was determined she could get you to listen to her before you'd listen to him?'

'I get the feeling you're about to enlighten me.'

'Yes, indeed I am.' She walked back towards the sofa, waving a hand as she went past him. 'Help yourself to beer, wine, coffee, whatever. You know where everything is.'

Tempting as a drink was, Connor decided against it.

Somehow he had a feeling that he was going to have to keep his wits about him. So he turned around and sat opposite her, his elbows on his knees while his errant eyes made an intensive study of her legs as she folded them back up on the sofa again.

He was definitely a legs man. And Shannon had *great* legs. Long, shapely, soft-skinned legs. And, as always, the sight of them reminded him of those legs wrapped around his while he pushed deep inside her body. Which would lead to the memory of her crying out his name, her sighs, her body tightening round his and pulling him over the edge.

Like last night, and every night since the night they had sorted through those few things.

When he smiled, her hand appeared in his line of vision, drawing the blanket back over her knees. And when his gaze rose to her face he saw a flush on her cheeks and a frown between her eyes. She knew what he was thinking. But she wasn't happy he was thinking it.

And Connor wondered if it was because she was annoyed at his sense of timing, his one-track mind, or just bugged by whatever his darling brother had said.

Any thought he might have had about finding out which one it was was abruptly interrupted by the frustrated edge to her voice.

'You know, if you stopped being such a moron for five minutes and answered the phone when he called you I wouldn't even have to have this damn conversation with you. I hate that there's still one of them that you haven't spoken to.'

'You don't have to have this conversation. Rory should never have asked you to get involved. And frankly I'd be much happier if you didn't get stuck in the middle.'

She shook her head in annoyance. 'He didn't ask me to get

involved. He came looking for you 'cos Mal told him where to find you. And since you weren't answering the phone—'

'I'm not ready to talk to him.' He frowned hard at the confession. 'I've already built plenty of bridges this last while. I'll get round to him. And if he didn't ask you to get involved, then why—?'

The outburst caught him unawares. '*Someone* had to tell you what an idiot you're being!'

And there was the *something* again. Way more obvious than it had been in a long time—and laced with a raw anguish that startled him.

'Shannon—'

'Do you know *why* he's been calling you more this last couple of weeks? No, of course you don't, because *you* don't answer the phone. Well, I'll just tell you why he's been calling—'

'I know—'

'No, *you don't!*' She leaned forwards, her eyes flashing in the soft light. 'Because you think he wants to try and force some kind of mutual admission of guilt on you that you're not up for. When all he wants to do is tell you that you're going to be an uncle!'

The statement momentarily silenced him. Because he knew what it would mean to his brother and his wife, hell, what it would mean to the whole family. It was a major event, the first of a new generation of Flanaghans.

When he didn't answer her straight away, Shannon made her own interpretation of his scowl and unfolded her legs again, to lean forward and ask him in a voice laced with emotion, 'How can that not matter to you? *How,* can you be this stupidly stubborn?'

The tears forming in her flashing eyes held all of Connor's attention. She looked as if he had somehow deeply hurt *her* by not talking to Rory. But that couldn't be right. So what in hell was wrong?

He felt an angry bubble of frustration building in his chest. Was she ever going to completely trust him? Hadn't they already proved how great they were together—how their lives had slotted so neatly around each other's? It all made perfect sense to *him.*

In the silence, the calm edge she forced into her voice was all the more noticeable to him. She was drawing back again, shutting herself off, forcing whatever pained her down inside as she always did. Where he supposedly wouldn't see it. 'You have such an amazing family and you've always been so close—even with Rory, who was away so much. How can you not know how very lucky that makes you, Connor?'

Suddenly part of her motivation in being so upset about the fight he'd had with his brother, even the earlier rift that he had had with the rest of his family until he'd started making amends of late, made more sense to him. And he mentally kicked himself for not piecing it together earlier. It wasn't as if she hadn't hinted at it before.

'I know you didn't have a big family growing up—' he took a deep breath before he continued '—and maybe I do need to talk with Rory, especially now—'

'Maybe?'

Keeping calm and avoiding another of their famous arguments was the least he could do this time, considering he knew her history, her way of building a substitute family within the walls of this building that she loved so much and considering that he knew she was only interfering because she cared.

He could give a little under those circumstances. 'All right. I do need to talk to him.'

Her green eyes widened marginally in surprise at his back-down. Then they narrowed in suspicion. 'Sooner rather than later.'

Connor smiled a half-smile. 'You're pushing it now. I'd suggest you quit while you're ahead.'

The very visible rise of her chin made him smile all the more. Until she eventually announced, 'You needn't try turning on the charm either. Because I know on top of everything else, you lied to me way back at the start.'

His smile left, at speed. 'Did I now?'

'Yes, you did. And you know you did.' When he simply stared at her with the same implacable gaze he had worn that first day, she shook her head and rose from the sofa again. 'I don't know why you feel the need to pretend to be someone you're not, Connor, especially with me.'

As she stepped near to his chair he reached a hand out and grasped her wrist, his long fingers tight against her beating pulse. And she froze. Nothing more than the skipping beat against his fingertips betraying the fact that she was affected by his touch. But it was enough.

Enough to encourage him to lean back in the over-stuffed chair a little while his fingers relaxed, his thumb brushing back and forth against that beating pulse. And his eyes watched the movement, still fascinated by the velvety smooth softness of her skin, even after being able to touch it and kiss it so often. He remembered seeing his hand on the pale skin of her shoulders, on her flat stomach, cupping her beautiful breasts; most of all he remembered it framing her face, when she closed her eyes and kissed his palm. So many new memories now.

When he spoke his voice came out a little huskier than he'd planned. 'What did I lie about?'

'Did you tell so many that you don't remember which one it might be?'

The question forced him to think about that while his thumb continued to rub back and forth, his eyes still fixed on the movement. 'I didn't lie about the building, or owning Devenish or never forgetting that one night we had. I didn't lie about not knowing sometimes whether to strangle you or kiss you—though I do think I have a preference firmer in my mind on that one now…'

Her pulse fluttered again.

'You told me when you were angry and bitter that you were on that mission of yours to have all that money to retire with.'

The soft background music came to an end, and Connor could hear her breathing, the small, shallow breaths she was taking that told him she was still annoyed enough to try to resist the effect of his touch.

'Yes, but you know I've bought more properties than I've sold lately—'

And he had, *surprisingly.* He was even getting a kick out of it. Once he'd finally come to the conclusion that he couldn't change the past and that he had to try and find a way to deal with what had been handed to him. Though Devenish Enterprises was a very different company in his hands than it had been in Frank's—it had moved into the twenty-first century, to begin with.

Connor was quite proud of that achievement.

'But you lied about the money.'

'No.' He smiled laconically at her wrist. 'I definitely have the money. You've stuck with a bone fide multimillionaire. In all his glory.'

She paused, took a deeper breath. 'You were using great chunks of that money to set up trust funds for your younger brothers and sisters. And paying off the entire families mortgages, even when you refused to speak to a single one of them.'

'Yes. Though, in fairness, Rory wasn't best pleased when I tried to pay *his* off. He was, shall we say, *rude* to the agent I sent…' He flashed a grin up at her.

When she didn't speak, he tilted his head to look up into her eyes, while she looked down at him from beneath long lashes, a myriad of emotions crossing her expressive emerald-green eyes. And then she smiled.

She was beautiful.

'Were you trying to get me to hate you on purpose?'

He felt his gut tighten in response, his hand automatically mirroring the sensation on her wrist as he tugged her round to the front of the sofa and down onto his lap, easing back into the cushions as he wrapped his arms around her. 'I was possibly a tad irritated by you at the time. We've come a long way since then, don't you think?'

Her throat convulsed, her tongue swiping across her bottom lip before she answered him with another half-hidden tremor in her voice. 'I really hated your guts for a while.'

He'd probably hated himself a little at the time.

'I know you did.' He pulled her closer to him and she lifted her knees, her head tilted back against his arm so she could look up at him.

'You can be such a pain when you set your mind to it.' She found one of the gaps between the buttons on his shirt and threaded her fingers in to touch his skin. 'But you looked like the weight of the world had been lifted off your shoulders when you came back from seeing your mum—think how you'd feel if you sorted things out with Rory.'

'Maybe.' He leaned down, resting his chin on top of her head, his fingertips smoothing from her knee to the edge of her loose shorts while he took a deep breath. He guessed if she was ever going to trust him with that something she still hid from him, then he had to show that sharing was something he could do too. 'But there's a longer history in my dispute with Rory. It's part and parcel of why I was a man on a mission when I came here.'

The surprise sounded in her voice, her fingers already beginning to undo buttons. 'I thought this was just about the fight you had at your mother's. Rory said you were angry at the time, said a few things he didn't appreciate you saying to your mum, and that he hit you for it. I'd probably have done the same thing.'

Connor smiled a very small smile. 'Yes, well, that's certainly a very condensed version of what happened. I got the solicitor's letter that morning bringing me the glad tidings and Rory was there when I confronted her. She felt that I hadn't had any need to know because my dad had loved me like all of his kids. I said that every child had a right to know where he came from and that every father should know he had a child—which she obviously *partially* agreed on 'cos Frank had known about *me.* She then had to confess to both of us that, after Rory was born, she and Dad were so young that they couldn't deal with a baby and keep their marriage afloat, so they split up—and then when they got together again she was already pregnant with me. And I made a few snide remarks about secrets and why Dad had forgiven her. And what kind of a guy Frank must have been for never wanting to see me.

And Rory stepped in when Mum got upset. He hit me when I wouldn't stop asking questions—I hit him back. And then when he wrestled me out the door, we had—*words.*'

Shannon went still against him.

He glanced down at the top of her head. 'And none of that's anything either of us can do anything about. It happened.'

'It must have been awful.'

He considered lying so she wouldn't think less of him for his behaviour, but decided he'd rather be honest and have her mad at him for a while. 'It wasn't pretty. But then you know how I can be in an argument—I have a tendency to fight fire with fire.'

Shannon seemed to be undoing the buttons on his shirt absent-mindedly, while her thoughts remained elsewhere. 'Maybe standing on the outside looking in on a family like yours is what it takes for me to see how important it is to hang onto something that rare—with both hands—no matter what. You know you need to sort it out with Rory. You won't be happy 'til you do; I *know* you.'

The familiar, telltale scent of flowers that would always be Shannon surrounded him, filling his senses and clouding his thoughts as she slid her hand inside his open shirt, her fingertips tracing over his skin before she reached her other hand up to his face, tilting her head back as she drew him into a slow, tender kiss that didn't last anywhere near long enough as far as Connor was concerned. Then, her nose close to his, she stared him in the eye while she told him in a determined voice, 'You're very dumb sometimes for someone so smart. You were never any less a brother or a son. One mistake before you were born was never going to take that away. *Idiot.*'

It had just taken him a while to remember that.

'I was smart enough to keep coming back to fight with you. I happen to think that redeems some of my other mistakes.'

She smiled with a familiar glint of mischief in her eyes. 'Mmm, you're still a work in progress, though.'

'You'll just have to fight to keep me, then.' He angled his head and kissed her again. This time with the kind of hunger that never seemed sated with her. No matter how many times he kissed her or made love to her. Which was *plenty.* He took winning her over *very seriously.*

But when he lifted his head and her lashes flickered upwards, revealing her familiar eyes, she seemed to momentarily forget she had to keep covering the something and the green shadowed over, even while she smiled at him.

Connor had been through a dozen scenarios for what was behind that something, some of them too horrible for him to even consider. If someone had *physically* hurt her, he would kill him.

'You hungry?'

Connor smiled back. 'Not for food.'

'I give up—you're officially insatiable.'

'You love that I'm insatiable, you know you do.'

Another long, hot kissing session, and they both scrambled to their feet, bedroom bound. And Connor's mind wandered along the way. If somewhere there *was* a man who had broken her heart to the extent that it held her back from loving again—then Connor was determined to make love to her again and again and again. Until that memory was erased from her mind and her heart. Then maybe she would tell him what had happened, and he would hold her and tell her that it would never happen again. He wouldn't let it. It was as simple as that.

Then his phone rang.

CHAPTER FOURTEEN

'HOW IS SHE?'

Connor's voice sounded tired on the other end of the line. 'She's fine. Doctor's looked at her again this morning and she's home now, surrounded by people fussing over her—which she hates.'

Shannon smiled. 'I bet. You'd hate it too, so that must be where you get it from. And they reckon it was just an angina attack?'

'Yeah, a warning, they say. But that's the second warning in three years so she has to start and behave. I think the excitement of being a grandmother was maybe too much. Cara says she has been running herself ragged buying baby things already. She'll have kittens when it gets here at this rate.'

And there it was again—the twisting agony inside her. She wanted so badly to be able to deal better with someone else's good news—but it had taken every ounce of strength she had in her to smile when Rory had beamed down at her as he'd told her about his baby.

By the time Connor had come home to her, she had managed to get herself calmer. But she had still had to fight to keep the pain of old from him—and it had been getting tougher to do every day as it was. Each day she spent with him, every night that she spent in his arms, made it more and more difficult to face the prospect of losing him.

'Where'd you go?'

She smiled, even though she knew she didn't have to force a smile when he couldn't see her. 'I'm here. So you're at the house now?'

'Nope—I'm on my way back. Should be there in just over an hour.'

'You're not staying?'

'She's kicking us all out, one by one. I didn't get a choice. And anyway—maybe I missed you.'

Her breath caught. Hell, but she had missed him too—big style. All night long she had tossed and turned, caught between horrible nightmares and periods of staring into the darkness. She couldn't hold it back from him any longer. Already she had stolen more time from him than she had a right to. And he didn't need her to remind him of how he used to be any more. He was already the man she had loved ten times over—slipping into the role of property developer with an enthusiasm that had made her so very proud of him.

But she couldn't stop herself from digging herself a little deeper in. 'Well, maybe I missed you too. There was no one here to make coffee first thing.'

Connor chuckled. 'Good thing too. No one makes coffee the way I do or wakes you up the way I do.'

Shannon smiled affectionately. 'Don't go over the speed limit, you idiot.'

'Too late.' He chuckled in return. 'I can't miss the lead-up to the big party tomorrow night, now, can I?'

'Not when you're the guest of honour—no.'

'Well, there you go, then. I'll see you soon.'

Shannon stood in the empty pottery room for a long while, listening to the bustle of people in the foyer. The party was the official opening night of the brand-new revamped community centre, but, while she was filled with joy and immense pride for all that Connor had done to make it happen, she also felt physically sick, mentally drained, as if she were carrying the weight of the world on her shoulders at the prospect of finally telling him what she had been holding back.

That was what someone got for holding back the truth for so long, she supposed. And the truth was she had probably used up all the strength she had trying not to love Connor any more than she already did. Not that that had worked. Because either side of the short bouts of depression she'd been suffering the last couple of weeks she had been ridiculously happy.

She was still trying to think of when would be the right time to tell him what was long overdue as she got ready for the party, rehearsing the words in her head and trying to keep busy to hide how much even thinking of saying them was hurting her. She was lugging away the last of the boxes and running up and down ladders to put streamers up—hauling one particularly heavy box when she cramped up.

The pain was sharp, taking her breath away.

'You'll pull a muscle like that.' Mario grasped hold of the other end of the box. 'After three. One, two, *three*—'

The second cramp doubled her, her arm automatically circling her stomach as she looked up at Mario's concerned face. 'No—'

He was at her side in a split second, his arm around her shoulders. 'I told you you'd pull something. You're a strapping lass, my precious, but you're no weightlifter.'

But Shannon could already feel tears welling in the backs of her eyes. Suddenly the way she had been feeling lately couldn't be put down entirely to her guilt, could it?

'I need you to take me to the hospital.'

'Does it feel that bad?' He laughed down at her. 'Everything still looks attached to me—'

'Please!' She grasped hold of his arm, looking up at him as the tears blurred her vision, her voice an anguished whisper. 'I think I might be having a miscarriage.'

Connor stood in the open doorway looking in on Shannon sitting on the edge of the bed, her eyes wide and unblinking, her nose and cheeks red—from crying? And he was torn between wanting to sweep her into his arms or turning round to go for another long walk up and down the disinfectant-scented corridors to get his own emotions under control.

Instead he stayed frozen to the spot until she took a shuddering breath, reaching up to wipe her eyes again, and she caught sight of him from her peripheral vision.

When she didn't speak he walked in and sat down on the bed beside her. 'Mario rang me. I let him go on—said I'd bring you home.'

'Okay.' She didn't manage to look him in the eye when he turned his face towards her. 'What did he tell you?'

'He told me.' Connor had never felt so inadequate, each word taking more effort than he had ever put into talking before, especially with Shannon, and especially after their last few weeks together.

'I wasn't pregnant.'

She said the words on that flat tone that he knew meant she had closed off again. And the swift shard of pain in his chest snapped him out of his own thoughts and into action, drawing her into his arms and kissing her hair before he asked in a husky voice, 'Are you upset you weren't?'

A part of him really needed to know whether having his child was something she would want too. It would have been fine with him—she'd have been bound to him then. And he wanted that. He wanted her inexorably tied to him. With no more doubts.

But he was glad she hadn't lost their child. It would have hurt unbearably if she'd miscarried and he'd have had to hide that from her while she needed him to be strong. That was another part of the man's job, after all, wasn't it? Through thick and thin—for better or for worse…

The thought surprised him. But it shouldn't have, not really. He'd known for a while.

With his head turned, his chin resting on the soft curls of her hair, he listened to her choked answer.

'The timing probably isn't right.'

'Maybe not. It's something we've not talked about either. After this, maybe we should…'

He let the suggestion hang in the air between them, giving her time to figure out that he was open to the idea of them having a family in the future.

But she went stiff in his arms.

'Yes, we should. It's a long overdue talk.' When she pulled out of his hold and stood up—reaching for her sweater in a room that already felt like a sauna to Connor—he frowned, watching her push each arm into a sleeve, pulling her head through, reaching up to free the long hair she had trapped.

Was she going to tell him that she didn't want to have kids with him some day? But Shannon loved kids. She worked with kids every damn day. And if she loved kids and still didn't want them with him, then did that mean she didn't love him? Or that she simply didn't love him enough yet to even think about it?

And if that was the case then what would it take to get her to feel that way?

Her eyes rose and locked with his across the narrow space between them. And with a jolt so strong it almost knocked him into next week—*Connor suddenly knew.*

He had no reason to know, but he knew—because the *something* was written on her face as clear as day. Not hidden. Not even an attempt made at hiding it from him.

He swore. 'You lost a baby before, didn't you?'

Shannon stared at him for a long while, her arms wrapping around her waist as if she was still cold—in a hot room with a sweater on.

Then she looked over his shoulder. And nodded.

Connor thrust himself upright, his words coming out on a wave of frustration. 'What about the baby's father—wasn't he there for you? Tell me you didn't go through that alone!'

Shannon visibly baulked, stepping back from him so that her back was pressed against the wall, her eyes wide with what Connor immediately recognized as—fear. She tilted her head, pursing her lips together as she stared at him with tears brimming over her bottom lashes.

This wasn't the Shannon he knew—the one who had fought him off for so long, the one who had taken on the woes of a building full of people, the one who met him halfway in everything, and then some. *Why* would she be afraid to tell him? Unless.

His heart stopped. *No.*

But before he could ask the question a nurse appeared

through the open doorway, staring at both of their faces with a curious expression before she smiled at Shannon and handed her a slip of paper.

'That's your prescription, Miss Hennessey. Plenty of fluids as well and you should shift the end of that bug you have.' She turned her attention to Connor. 'And make sure she doesn't go trying to lift something that heavy again too, won't you?'

Connor nodded dumbly.

So Shannon stepped in, filling the silent void with the obvious question. 'I can go now?'

'Yes, just make sure you visit your GP.'

'I will.'

Connor stepped back, allowing her to go through the door ahead of him, neither of them speaking until the lift doors swished shut.

Where he finally asked the question that was burning like acid in the pit of his stomach. 'You didn't have heatstroke when you were in hospital in the States, did you?'

He didn't look at her as the doors opened on another floor, an elderly man stepping in to join them as Shannon managed a small-voiced, 'No, I didn't.'

The elderly man got out a floor before them, where they were joined by two nurses. And Connor frowned at the intrusion. But he didn't want to hear what Shannon had to say in a lift or in the car park. Taking her back home wasn't an option either—not with the last of the party preparations ensuring there would be a crowd to hear what they were talking about.

It was entirely too personal for that.

So when they stepped out of the lift he grasped her elbow in a firm hold, his calm tone not even hinting at the myriad of conflicting emotions he currently felt.

'We'll go to my hotel.'

Shannon nodded in silence, her chin rising so that he knew she was preparing herself for confrontation.

So, to make sure she was in no doubt whatsoever, he leaned in closer to add, 'And no more lies—nothing held back. I *mean* it.'

Shannon endured the awful silence between them in the car as Connor guided them through Friday-night traffic to the hotel. Her eyes fixed on her reflection in the side window and beyond to the faces of all the smiling, laughing people in the streets heading out for a night of fun in bars and nightclubs. Their lives looked so simple in comparison to where hers was now. Smiling, laughing, happy—the polar opposites of everything she was feeling.

But she had known this day would come. Hadn't she?

'No more lies,' Connor had said.

The hotel was way too expensive for her to have ever visited before, but she didn't even glance at the marbled columns or the beautiful bouquets of flowers that scented the air around them. She didn't even look at Connor as he strode purposefully through the giant foyer, nodding to the concierge who greeted him by name.

But she was so very conscious of the fact that this was Connor's new world. It was almost representative of the vast distance between them.

She, who had been happy, she'd thought, building a simple life, surrounded by warm people who had welcomed her into their lives without any questions or explanations of what had happened before she'd met them. Connor, who, although he was still finding his feet in his new life, had only taken a temporary break in that world, until he found out what had happened before, when he would leave and step straight back into this new world, wouldn't he?

She'd been a rabbit in the headlights since he'd come back, hadn't she?

Still hugging her arms tightly around her waist, she glanced briefly around the pristinely clean room with its perfectly co-ordinated soft furnishings. Then down at her loose sweater, worn jeans, and tattered trainers.

'Were you *ever* planning on telling me?'

She straightened as Connor's voice sounded close behind her, the strain in his voice clear.

'Yes.' It was the truth, whether he chose to believe it or not. Finding the right time had been the biggest problem of all even when it had happened—finding the right time in the here and now to right the wrong that had been done so long ago, twice as hard. And letting him go the main reason she couldn't bring herself to do it since she had had him back again and discovered that how she felt about him was stronger than it had been before.

So much for the theory she'd had on seven-year cycles!

'What about back then, Shannon? Did it occur to you that I might have wanted to know I was going to be a father?'

'Yes.' It had more than occurred to her. But the simple fact was, she hadn't told him, and then it had been too late. Their baby had been dead and she had been alone.

Connor appeared in front of her, grasping her elbow in a similar hard hold to the one he had used when they had come out of the lift at the hospital. And he looked so angry, so dis-appointed in her—

It opened the dam inside her as he swore viciously beneath his breath.

But what had she expected? It was an echo of the pain he'd felt when he'd found out about his own father. And he'd been so very angry about that.

'Then why didn't you? Did you think I wouldn't care—that I wouldn't want to know—that I wouldn't *be there?*'

She snatched her elbow free. 'You think I didn't want you there? As far as I knew, you didn't even know it was me that night! How was I supposed to call you out of the blue and announce you were going to be a father?'

'By picking up the phone! I *knew* it was you!'

'*I* didn't know that!' Her voice cracked as tears spilled over her lashes, any semblance of control she had left evaporating. 'And if you think that I didn't want you there then you have no idea how much I used to love you! I loved you so much that leaving you almost killed me—but I only *thought* I knew what it felt like to die inside. I only *thought* I knew how much one person could hurt to lose someone until—until—the second that—until—'

She turned away in frustration as words failed her. Because she needed him to understand. And in order to do that she needed to be as clear and lucid as possible.

Connor was staring at her with what looked like horror on his face when she finally looked at him again. Then he scowled hard, shaking his head as he began to pace in front of her, which gave her time to take deep, shaking breaths while she swiped the tears off her face with her palms.

When she spoke again, she had almost managed to put the flat tone back into her voice—almost. Only the odd word shook when she spoke.

'I was so miserable when I got there. I don't think I had dealt with my nan's death, and then there was leaving you—

even though I knew I had to leave you—winning the scholarship for that course was my only chance to try and make a life for myself. I just wanted that one night. I wanted to be with you—because I didn't want someone else the first time. I didn't want it to be someone I didn't love.' She took another long breath. 'And it was, it was—'

'Yes, *it was*. And yet the first thing you said when I saw you again was how much you'd regretted it. How it had been the worst mistake you ever made.'

The fact that his tone had changed from frustrated to husky tore her in two inside, so that her attempt at control started to slip again. 'Because I knew what the outcome of it was. I can never, ever think about that night without thinking of all the pain that came after it.'

Connor's jaw clenched hard, so that he spoke from between gritted teeth. 'I want to know all of it. Every single bit. When did you miscarry?'

The sob came from low inside her, from the dark place where the agony still lived. 'I didn't miscarry.'

The pacing stopped immediately, all the colour draining from his gorgeous face.

Shannon turned her head so that she couldn't see the torment in his eyes, her gaze focusing on the empty middle distance as she rhymed off the details with a series of shuddering breaths, sobs, and occasional wiping of her cheeks with the end of one sleeve of her sweater.

'I did have heatstroke when I got there. I was sick for weeks one way or another. And I thought it was because I was so tired and so miserable. They kept us on the go all the time at the activity centre—swimming, hiking, trampolining, abseiling. It never once occurred to me—I mean—I just thought

I'd messed up my cycle—I never thought. And then—when I knew—it was like I'd been given this amazing gift. I had a part of you inside me. I could have a family again—someone I could love without trying to hide how I felt. I rehearsed a dozen different ways of telling you—I wrote letters—'

'I never got any letters.'

'I didn't send them.'

'Why not?'

She blinked away the fat tears on her lower lashes, risking a quick glance at him while wiping her cheeks again. 'I'd been talking to Tess and she told me you were seeing someone.'

Connor frowned hard. 'Who was I seeing?'

'I don't know—Sharon someone.'

He swore again.

'I tore the letters up. I told myself that I couldn't tell you if you were already seeing someone else. It wouldn't be fair. It would be like I was trapping you.'

He swore again.

And Shannon grimaced at the sound of each sharp expletive. 'When I heard you weren't seeing her any more I wanted to tell you then but—'

When she fought to hold back an uncontrollable bout of savage sobbing, Connor stepped in closer. *'But?'*

It took several moments before she could speak, her arms wrapped firmly round her waist as she gave up on wiping her cheeks and instead tried to hold the debilitating cramping agony inside where she had locked it all this time.

'He stopped moving. He stopped moving and for days I didn't think there was anything wrong. But he had stopped moving—and when I went—when I saw the doctor—he said…'

She took a massively large breath and choked out the rest. 'He told me that it was too late. The baby, he had—well, his heart—you see, it had stopped beating. And I had to go all the way through labour knowing that I wouldn't have a baby—our baby—at the end of it. Because he was already dead.'

CHAPTER FIFTEEN

IT WAS TOO MUCH to watch Shannon's pain, take it all in, and deal with his own emotions as he processed it all. Connor had promised himself that he would kill whoever it was had hurt her so badly, when all along it had been him.

He had caused her this pain because he hadn't fought to keep her when he should have.

In the midst of the conflicted emotions he felt, he found only one question to force out. '*He?* The baby was a "he"?'

She nodded.

And Connor badly wanted to throw something. To shout and yell at the unfairness of never having been told so that he'd have had a chance to be there.

But just how much Shannon had already suffered was written all over her—in her glistening eyes; in the almost translucent paleness of her face; in the hunch of her shoulders, and the stance she had adopted hugging her arms around herself. She was trying to hold the something inside the way she had all along.

Since the day she had watched him with the kids in her group. When she must have looked at him with them and thought of the child she had lost.

The something had to be agonizing. It was hell for him and he hadn't lived through it.

For better or for worse.

That was the decision he'd already made, wasn't it? And this definitely fell into *worse*. Connor couldn't think of anything worse.

Enough was enough. So, with a low groan, he stepped forwards and hauled her into his arms, crushing her to him. When she struggled, he held tighter, when she finally succumbed and sobbed against his shirt, he looked to the heavens for strength to be the man she needed him to be.

She should never have had to go through it alone, 'I should have been there.'

Her head shook back and forth against him, lifting back a little so he could hear her words. 'I never gave you the choice. It was my fault, Connor—all of it. And if we hadn't ended up together again I don't know that I could ever have searched you out to tell you. And that makes me as much of a liar as everyone else who has hurt you this last while by keeping secrets. I should never have let this happen with us again. But I couldn't stop it.'

'I didn't give you a big choice this time round. It's what I should have done the first time. But you sneaked out in the middle of the night and I never got a chance to talk to you again. I let my pride get in the way.'

'I couldn't take a chance on you figuring out it was me—'

'That didn't go so well.'

'I know that now. But I didn't then.' She sniffed, and he could hear in her voice that she was getting back some of her control—though her voice was lacking that deathly calm, emotionless edge that he had learned to hate so much lately. 'But it wouldn't have stopped me I don't think—from leaving, I mean. I thought about it from so many different angles after I'd left. And it didn't matter what had happened—you didn't feel the way I did. I'd have told you if—I'd have let you know if—'

Connor tightened his arms around her, reassuring her that he understood without her having to say the words. 'I wish you had told me. I won't say that I don't. But it was seven years ago, Shannon. It can't be changed.'

Finally her arms reached up to circle his waist, wrapping around and holding on equally tight as he held her while she pressed her cheek against his shirt, directly above his heart. 'I wanted you there. So much. I can't tell you how much. After it happened, when I was alone—'

'Stop.' He squeezed his arms again.

'No.' Her head rose and she looked up at him with her large green eyes filling with tears again. 'I want you to know everything Connor. All of it.'

And as difficult as it would be to hear, he wanted to know all of it. So that there wouldn't be any more secrets between them. Without a doubt, as far as he was concerned, this was the beginning for them. It had to be done right. So he nodded.

After a moment, focusing on the hollow at the base of his throat, she took a breath and told him the rest. 'When it was all over, there was a long time when I didn't think I would ever get out of bed again. I wanted to die. But eventually I found a way to get through the day.' She glanced upwards from below lashes still thick with the diamond bright sparkles of her tears. 'It never goes away—the pain of it—it never does. And I don't think I remembered what it felt like to be really happy again until I came to Galway.'

Connor saw the tiny wistful smile when she looked up at

him again. 'When you found a family inside that run-down old building.'

'Yes.' The smile remained. 'I'd forgotten about the ability of the Irish to laugh and smile, no matter what life throws their way. And some of those people have had a much worse time than I had—have lost loved ones, fought through illness, had days when they had to scrape together enough money to feed their kids that night. And they still get together and laugh and tell jokes. They taught me that one person can get through more than they think they can. They're my family—every single one of them. And in that building I had my first real home in a very long time.'

'Until I came to take it away from you.'

A nod. 'Until you came to take it away from me.'

Now he knew why she had fought him so hard at the beginning. It had taken him a long time to understand even half of it, but now that he had the whole story…

'It makes sense now.'

Her hands smoothed up his back as she loosened her hold on him a little. 'At first I felt like it was some kind of punishment. I don't expect that you'll understand that, but it was how it felt. And I fought that—especially when you were so—'

'Disagreeable?' He raised an eyebrow.

'Well, yes. I just thought, no, I've paid for my mistakes for so long. I can't keep paying for them.'

'And I don't want you to either—let's just get that clear. You went through all that on your own—that's more than enough punishment. But you're not the only one who made mistakes.'

Oh, no, because Connor could see everything clearly now. Suddenly everything made sense. Like the pieces of a puzzle slotting into place. *Finally.*

But his words seemed to stir up more pain, her voice cracking again. 'But it *was* my fault. No matter what way you look at it—what happened to our baby was my fault. If I'd known sooner—if I'd taken better care of myself—if I'd noticed he'd stopped moving sooner—'

'Stop.' He hauled her in tight again. 'Stop doing that, Shannon. I mean it. Sometimes things are just beyond our control. It's the way it is and nothing we can do now can change it. You can't live your whole life torturing yourself over it any more than I can change things and go back to stop you from leaving in the first place. What happened, happened. All we can do is try and make things right from here on in.'

Yes, he'd learnt a lot this last few months, hadn't he? And most of it due to her.

Her head tilted back, green eyes wide with stark astonishment. 'How can you say that? How can you forgive me for keeping all this from you, especially after everything you've been going through this last while? What I did—by not telling you—is just as bad as the secret your mother kept from you. You were so very angry with her. And even knowing that I still allowed myself to get involved with you—because when it comes to you I just can't seem to stop myself. It's always been that way. *Always*. And the number of times when you made love to me and held me and I still couldn't find the words to tell you…'

As her words tickled away into silence he saw how all he had said and done recently had to have added to her sense of guilt and her pain. She had been holding back from him since they'd got back together because he had given her no choice. He had walked into her life, threatened to take away the one place that meant something to her after years of being unhappy and alone, and then he had gone on and on about being lied to, his sense of betrayal, his anger at his family—no matter how much he loved them.

Yet even while he had been unwittingly making things worse, she had still fought the bit out with him to make him see sense, to yell at him about the way he was behaving, to allow him—despite what she thought—with *considerable* persuasion back into her life, and to then encourage him to build bridges with the people that loved him.

She had done all of that—*for him.* Did she think he would push her away after all that? Didn't she know what it had been like for him without her?

'There's something you need to know about that time when I was so angry at the world. We need everything from those missing seven years out in the open. And now that you've bared your soul to me I want to tell you. Because I do know about that sense of being punished for something. It was how I felt when the letter came from Frank's solicitors.'

A small vertical line appeared between her shining eyes, confusion written all over her face. 'What did you feel you had to be punished for?'

He managed to tear his gaze from hers, looking around the large suite he had barely spent any time in for weeks now before he unwrapped his arms from her slender frame to take her hand and lead her to a sofa. 'Over here.'

And she followed without any resistance—trusting him enough to sit down at his side, to allow her hands to be folded in his where they lay on her lap.

Damn, but he loved this woman. And all of the strength it had taken her to get where they were now.

'When we had that big row the night of the museum do,

we both threw at each other the fact that there were things that had happened when we were apart, remember?'

'I remember. That was the sex-versus-making-love issue night.'

'Yes.' He smiled slowly. 'Now that you've told me about your missing seven years, I'm going to do the same. And when I'm done you'll realize that I've been just as miserable without you as you've been without me. The reason all this happened was because we weren't honest with each other back then—that's not going to happen this time.'

Two more silent tears dropped slowly off the end of her lashes, trickling down her cheeks, mesmerizing him. And in that moment he vowed to himself that those would be the last. Tonight would be the last time she would have to cry about anything wrapped up in their relationship. Past, present, or future.

'I don't think I understood what had been wrong with me until I saw you again. Being with you has made sense of it.' He took a breath to give himself time to get it all straight. 'I was angry for a long time before that letter even came. You left—and I spent years being angry and resentful about that. I thought you had played me. And I swore that would never happen again. I would never get sucked into something that wasn't solely on my terms. Rory was always the responsible one—he took that kind of thing on for everyone, it was just in him. I think he flourished under it. But he also got to go away and do what he wanted to do, which left the responsibilities at home on my shoulders. And I did it. But I resented him for it. I thought that he got to breeze back and forth playing some kind of hero while I got to sit at home and keep everything ticking along in his absence. He forced a life on me I didn't want.'

'I thought you enjoyed running the gyms? You did such a good job of them. Tess was never done singing your praises.'

'I did enjoy it. But I was restless. Rory was out in the Middle East doing something he believed in and I felt trapped by the responsibility he left behind. We even argued about it when he got sent home the time he was injured and met Cara. And I even felt jealous of him for that—everything seemed so easy for him. He got to join the army when he wanted to, live a well-paid adventure when he wanted to, meet someone he could spend the rest of his life with at just the right time for him to come home and settle down. And I resented the hell out of him for that. So, when the letter came and we argued—a lot of that came spilling out while I was so angry. Suffice to say—it wasn't as easy for him as I'd always thought it was. I was wrong. I had to apologize to him for that when I saw him last night.'

Shannon turned her small hands inside his, her fingers weaving with his before she gave them a squeeze of encouragement. 'Go on.'

He took another breath, looking up into her eyes, 'To me, finding out I wasn't a part of the family the way I'd thought I was was like some kind of punishment for not realizing what I had. I'd been so resentful of how restless I'd felt for so long that I needed a kick in the ass to make me think straight. And then, when I saw you, I think I knew. It just took me a while to figure it out. I guess at the end of the day I have Frank McMahon to thank, ironically. If he hadn't left me that building I might never have met you again. And then I might never have known the truth.'

Her breath caught, her voice a whisper. 'Which is?'

'That I'd spent all that time missing you. I should never

have let you go—I should have followed you over there and dragged you back. And now that I know what you went through without me, I'm all the more certain that that's what I should have done. Then we could have spent those seven years together and not had to put each other through all this, this time round.'

Untangling one hand, he lifted it to the side of her face, smiling when she leaned into his palm as his fingers threaded into her hair. 'You were wrong about how I felt. I loved you then, Shannon, I should have told you that but I always assumed you knew. And the fact that you knew and still left killed me. I walked around for months angry at you. Then I dated Sharon for a while to try and forget you. But it was too soon. So I buried myself in the work I resented and became a serial dater for a while. But none of them were you. I never loved anyone else the same way.'

Shannon's answer was anguished. 'I didn't know Connor, I swear. If I'd known I wouldn't have left.'

'And if I'd known then that *you* loved *me* I wouldn't have given you a choice. We both got it wrong. And we've both paid a price for getting it that wrong. Now we've got a chance to put it right again.'

More tears fell down her cheeks, some of them into his palm where her cheek was nestled, so he brushed them away with his thumb, leaning in closer to her to continue in a low voice.

'You still love me, Shannon Hennessey. I know you do. Because ever since I found you again you've done nothing but force me to think about the kind of person I'd become. To make me open my eyes and see what was really worth hanging onto. And you did that even though every day with me reminded you of what you went through on your own. You love me. And, like you said, I'm still a work in progress, so there's no way I'm letting you go again. I need you.'

Her answering smile was as bright as her nickname of old. 'Yes, I still love you. I never stopped, even when loving you hurt, even when I hated you—I never stopped. All this while I've been convinced that when I told you everything I would lose you. And I would have understood that. But I wanted to hold onto you for as long as I could. Because I love you more now than I did then. I was young then. Now I'm all grown up and I know better how hard it is to find something like this.'

Releasing his other hand, he framed her face, leaning in closer to inform her in no uncertain terms, 'You won't lose me. Get that straight. You've got me. You had me again at that first dumb T-shirt. And as to you being scared—*nah.*' He shook his head. 'You're the bravest woman I know. You went through all of that on your own when you didn't have to and you came out the other side and still took a chance on us again.'

'Well, I did try for a while to keep you at arm's length but you wouldn't let me, remember?'

'And why do you think that might be?'

The way that her gorgeous eyes shimmered at him told him that she knew the answer now.

So he leaned in further and claimed her mouth, tasting the saltiness on her lips from her tears as he kissed the last of them away.

And the familiar heat between them fired immediately; as if all of the confessions had somehow seeded a deep need in them to finally let out in one go all the emotion that they had been holding back.

Connor kissed the corners of her mouth, her cheeks, her eyes, her forehead, down the side of her face to the neck she automatically tilted his way, while she told him again, 'I love you, Connor Flanaghan.'

He leaned back long enough to pull her sweater over her head, before he kissed her again, the words husky against her mouth.

'And I love you. I've been trying to show you how much this last while by making love to you every chance I got. I don't know how you didn't know that.'

Shannon lifted her hands and framed his face, her eyes filled with emotion. 'Show me again and I promise I'll listen this time.' She took a breath. 'But I don't want anything between us again. I want a baby with you, Connor. Not to replace the one we lost, 'cos that'll never happen. But I want children with you. I want us to have a family. I know that's not maybe what a lot of people our ages want, but I don't care.'

'Then we'll just stay in bed until we make one.' He leaned his forehead against hers. 'All that time when I knew there was something you were holding back from me I thought that it was that you'd fallen in love with someone else and he had broken your heart. So I decided I would spend as long as it took getting you to trust me and love me. Even earlier on, when I was being such a pain, I kept coming back to argue with you and listen to everything you threw at me—even when I didn't realize why I kept coming back. But somewhere inside I knew why I was doing it. I wasn't letting you go again. I'm never letting you go again. We're going to get married and have dozens of kids and we'll find a house and live happily ever after. It's just that simple.'

Her hands rose to rest on his against her face, her voice back to the confident tone that he loved. 'Yes, to all of those things. I want to spend the rest of my life with you—making love and arguing and making up and laughing and doing all the things that other couples who love each other do. I want you to bring bags of Dolly Mixtures for us to eat on film nights—like the boiled sweets that old man in front us that night does every week for his wife, and has done every Friday night for forty years.'

Connor's smile grew. 'You didn't tell me that.'

'I thought you'd read something into it at the time—having just done the same thing for me. When you remembered them that night I think I knew then that I wasn't going to be able to resist you this time round. It frightened the life out of me. So I tried pushing you away again. But you wouldn't go. And I couldn't resist when you wouldn't go.'

'I'm irresistible. That's basically what you're saying?'

'Heaven help me—yes it is.'

'Good.' He kissed her again, long and slow, feeling her lean into him as his body started to tighten with need. So he lifted his mouth an inch from hers to tell her, 'Then let's start right now with making that family. As one of six I have a tradition to uphold.'

'And then we can go to the party tomorrow night and tell Mario he's going to get his wish to be a bridesmaid…'

'The hell we will.'

Shannon laughed, the sound warming his heart in a way it hadn't been warmed in seven years. She was his. For better or worse. Together they could get through anything. Apart they were both giant big train wrecks.

Maybe that was part of what that dumb film he'd watched with her had been about? Who knew?

As he stood and tugged her to her feet, his eyes dropped to the message on her T-shirt. And when he looked at her face, she was lifting her chin, obviously having read it herself.

She grinned at him. 'It's my favourite one.'

Connor read it again: 'Here I am. Now what are your other two wishes?'

He laughed, leaning in to kiss her soundly again as he led her to the huge bed on the other side of the room. 'I need one that says "Marry me and make love every day for the rest of our lives."'

Shannon was already reaching for the buttons on his shirt. 'Then I'll need one that says "Yes to all of the above."'

And Connor proceeded to show her he was very happy with that answer.

The slow and torturous way.

NIROLI/LIST/1-4

...International affairs, seduction and passion guaranteed

Volume 1 – July 2007
The Future King's Pregnant Mistress by Penny Jordan

Volume 2 – August 2007
Surgeon Prince, Ordinary Wife by Melanie Milburne

Volume 3 – September 2007
Bought by the Billionaire Prince by Carol Marinelli

Volume 4 – October 2007
The Tycoon's Princess Bride by Natasha Oakley

8 volumes in all to collect!